"This must be appallingly obvious."

She couldn't help smiling, and reached out again to reassure herself that he was real.

"It must," he agreed.

"How embarrassing!"

He grinned. "Don't worry, Janis. People are always nice to lovers."

Lovers, thought Janis. *I love him, yet I still can't trust him. And when he discovers what I've been doing on the design contracts, it's all so sure to fall to pieces.*

Her lips trembled, and Marcus, mistaking her thoughts, stilled them with another kiss.

English author **Sally Cook** lives in Norwich with her two small sons. She has been a professional writer for nine years, but only recently has branched into fiction. This is her first appearance in the Harlequin Romance line.

Takeover Bid

Sally Cook

Harlequin Books

TORONTO • NEW YORK • LONDON
AMSTERDAM • PARIS • SYDNEY • HAMBURG
STOCKHOLM • ATHENS • TOKYO • MILAN

Original hardcover edition published in 1988
by Mills & Boon Limited

ISBN 0-373-17025-4

Harlequin Romance first edition November 1988

CHAPTER ONE

'I THINK you should sell the company.'

Mr Anson had a very deep voice, warm-toned and velvety smooth, the kind of voice that washed over you, giving you a comforting sense of reassurance. Until you took in what he was actually saying.

That took Janis Trench a minute, since she had been only half listening to him up to then. A little shock went through her, and she jerked upright on the hard typist's chair. 'Sell?' she echoed, disbelievingly.

'Not that it would be saleable in its present form, as far as I can judge. In fact, there's something to be said for going into voluntary receivership.'

'Re——' Janis began, and then stopped dead as the full enormity of it struck her. She stared at him, open-mouthed. He was sprawling back, perfectly comfortably, in her chair, at her desk. He had crooked one long leg up, resting his foot on his other knee, and had leaned against it a pad of paper which was covered in his notes. He tapped this lazily with the tip of a Biro as he waited for her to reply.

'Are you trying to tell me,' she said in a very quiet, even voice, 'that we are going bankrupt?'

'Actually, it's quite impossible to tell at the moment. These books are in the most atrocious state I've seen for a long time.'

He met her look full on as he said this. He had dark eyes, and Janis found his gaze oddly disconcerting. She found everything about Mr Anson disconcerting.

5

He was arrogant and self-assured, he had taken over her office as if he owned it—and now he was making these unspeakable remarks about her company. And freely admitting he had no evidence to back them up!

Janis suddenly found she was very, very angry.

'In that case,' she retorted, 'you have absolutely no right to make that sort of allegation. We're doing very well, I'll have you know. We've kept almost all our major contracts since my father died. Of course we aren't bankrupt!'

'You do have a cash-flow crisis.'

That was a polite term for it. Trenco didn't have enough money to pay that month's wages and the urgent bills that were piling up. That was why Janis had been forced to turn to the bank; and the bank had commissioned Mr Anson, accountant, to check out the company's position before it agreed to lend her any more.

'Yes, we do,' Janis admitted, 'but that's because I knew we needed to invest in new machines, and . . .'

'And because you haven't brought in nearly as many small contracts as your father did, and because you didn't trouble to speak to Mr Jenkins at the bank before you went out to spend two thousand pounds that you didn't have.'

It was true, Janis thought, about the small contracts. How had he discovered that, when he claimed not to have been able to decipher the books at all? Telepathy, perhaps? It was something she had not let herself think about. Running Trenco by herself was difficult enough, without worrying about whether they really *were* going bankrupt. She had never even considered that before. It was a cash-flow crisis that they faced, that was what she had told herself. As for the other—it didn't bear contemplation, especially not while Mr Anson was watching her.

He had given her an escape route, though; and she used it.

'We would have had more than the two thousand pounds, if Trubrite hadn't gone into liquidation owing us six months' payments. I wasn't to know that was going to happen.' Mr Anson did not reply, and Janis added, defiantly, 'Was I?'

Mr Anson's mouth lifted slightly at the corners. 'No, you weren't, he agreed. 'And that is why I think you should sell the company.'

'But that could have happened to anybody! Every company suffers bad debts. It's just that this one happened at such an awkward time, and . . .'

Mr Anson broke in, inexorably. 'Now, Miss Trench, that isn't what I said. I said *you* were not to know about Trubrite. Considering the state of your books, that's perfectly true. But other managements would have known. If you had been analysing your contractors' payments properly, you would have seen that Trubrite were paying more and more slowly. And if you had read the financial press, or if you'd had closer contacts in the financial markets, you would have realised Trubrite were in deep trouble. Then you could have insisted that they paid their outstanding bills before you did any more work for them, and you wouldn't have lost nearly as much when they collapsed.'

Janis glared at him. It was difficult to think of an adequate retort to that reasoned argument. And she was uneasily conscious that it wasn't at all wise to shout at the accountant that the bank had sent in; especially when he wasn't shouting back at her at all—just sitting there, goading her, and waiting for her to make a fool of herself.

She clenched her fists tightly, and thought privately

about smashing one of them right into the middle of
Mr Anson's quite unreasonably handsome face.
Instead she forced a little smile, and said quietly,
'Look, Mr Anson, I do realise I've made some
mistakes. I suppose it's only inevitable that I should
have done, after taking over the running of the
company so suddenly, and with so little experience. I
do appreciate that the books aren't as tidy as they
might be, but I simply haven't had time to straighten
them out yet. The messy ledgers aren't hiding any real
problems, though, I promise you. This is just a
temporary crisis. I'll make sure it doesn't happen
again. Really, I'm sure Trenco is doing very well.'

'Would *you* feel that way, Miss Trench, if you had a
very substantial sum invested in this company?'

'I *do* have a lot invested in it,' Janis retorted. 'Not
just money, either. This is my life, Mr Anson. I'm
putting everything I have into it.'

'I don't question that, Miss Trench. But, if you
were the bank official in charge of company loans,
would *you* be satisfied that this company was well
run? Or that it was going to be run well in future?'

Janis leaped up from her seat. 'Now look here, Mr
Anson! You might not approve of young women
running companies, but that's no reason to assume
that every bank manager in the country is as much of
a male chauvinist as you are!'

'Mr Jenkins is considerably more of one, I promise
you.' Mr Anson's eyes looked her over, appraising her
slim figure, shamelessly contradicting his words.
Then he uncurled his legs and leaned forward,
suddenly businesslike. 'I wouldn't question your
ability if these books were in good order, or if you
were a trained accountant; even if you had a
qualification in business studies. But what are your

qualifications for running a company, Miss Trench?'
He looked disparagingly down at Janis's *curriculum
vitae*, spread out on the desk next to the offending
ledgers. 'A diploma in fashion design from Smithbury
Polytechnic!'

'That's a very relevant qualification for the head of
a clothing company. We'd soon go under if we
weren't able to judge fashion trends.'

'Not if you carried on like your father did, and concentrated on filling fixed orders for shirts from large
stores.'

'The store chains, too, are changing these days,'
Janis replied. 'They simply don't sell dozens of plain
white, blue and grey shirts in dull styles any more. Or,
if they do, they get them from Far Eastern
manufacturers at prices we couldn't possibly match.
They want fashionable clothes, original clothes.
Those are the only clothes they pay more than sub-
minimum rates for. And in a year or two, Trenco will
be geared up to producing them.'

'Sit down again, Miss Trench,' Mr Anson said.
'No, on second thoughts, why don't you go and ask
that secretary to make us both a strong cup of coffee?'

Janis glared at him. She could just imagine Anthea
tripping back in from the reception area where she
had been banished, and making eyes at Mr Anson
while she spooned the sugar into his coffee! 'I'll make
it myself,' she muttered, crossing over to the kettle on
the shelf in the corner.

'Black, no sugar.' He actually had the nerve to smile
at her as he said it. To punish him, Janis put two Rich
Tea biscuits on his saucer, where they would be sure
to go soggy if he didn't eat them. He ignored them
completely, she noticed, and launched back into the
attack without taking even a sip of the coffee.

Perhaps it was just as well, since she had heaped three spoonfuls of granules into the cup, and it was scalding hot!

'The bank agreed to lend your father money, Miss Trench, on the understanding that this was a long-established, low-risk company, producing goods not remotely subject to the freaks of fashion, on contract to a number of very reputable large companies. Trenco was just the kind of small firm that banks like. They wanted some security, of course, but nothing like as much as they would have demanded if Trenco had been a small fashion house trying to establish itself. Personally, I think old Jenkins would have been wise to send in an accountant at that stage, but presumably he felt he knew your father well enough to do without. Trenco must have looked like a very good risk then.'

'It's a good risk now,' Janis retorted.

'Is it? You don't merely want the bank to continue their loan—you want to increase it. Your accounts are a disaster area, you can't produce any kind of financial forecast to back up your assertions—and now you suddenly spring on me the fact that you plan to switch to a high-risk line of business!'

'It would be more of a risk to carry on as we were, for heaven's sake! That market's disappearing. My father saw it, too; he was planning to make just the change I'm now aiming for. My clothes aren't weird, they aren't way-out. They are just ordinary, wearable clothes—exactly what chain-store buyers want.'

'Can you prove that to me?'

'Not yet, but within a year I should be able to.' Janis leaned forward. 'I'm just asking for some time, Mr Anson. For a little understanding, a chance to get over the bad debt.'

Mr Anson, disconcertingly, responded by leaning closer to her. 'You're asking the wrong man, Miss Trench. I don't give understanding. The bank hired me to provide a factual report on the position and prospects of this company.'

'But you don't know enough about the clothing market to be able to judge our prospects!' Janis responded, despairingly.

'I can tell a well run company when I see one, though. And this——' Mr Anson tapped the pile of ledgers '—is not a sign of a well run company.'

'I'll start tonight. I'll work evenings on it, every night, until I get the books in order.'

Mr Anson shook his head. His dark hair flopped forwards into his eyes as he did so, and he reached out a hand to push it backwards. He had long hands, Janis couldn't help noticing, with straight fingers and well cut nails. His shirt cuff was double-stitched, a good European make, not any of the Far Eastern trash that was flooding the market, and his watch was a businesslike steel model.

'You simply don't understand what's needed. It isn't just a question of balancing the books. Your whole accounting system is hopelessly inadequate for a company of this type. You need a well qualified accountant, or an experienced book-keeper at the very least—somebody who can set up a decent system from scratch for you, and transfer over to it all this year's figures.'

Janis groaned. 'You know how impossible it is to find anyone like that, Mr Anson. And, even if we did find someone, we couldn't possibly afford to pay them.'

'Which is why you should think about going into receivership. Then your receivers would be paid directly from the assets of the company and, if there were any prospect of restructuring Trenco as a viable business, they would be in the best possible position to find you a buyer.'

Janis hesitated. There was something very tempting about the idea of selling Trenco, offloading all her worries. It wouldn't work, though. Maybe she would have to think harder about how the company was doing, where it was going; but she didn't have to think hard to realise that handing over to a receiver would be a financial disaster. Not only for her—she was young, she could stand it—but for her mother, too.

She couldn't possibly admit that to Mr Anson. Admit that White Gates was mortgaged to the limit as security for the bank loan, that doing as he suggested would most probably make herself and her mother homeless, with no income but the little Janis would be able to earn as a designer—she couldn't do that. She might have been tempted, if she had thought he would be understanding, but hadn't he already admitted that he had no intention of being understanding?

'I don't want to sell!' Her voice was growing louder again.

Mr Anson reached out his hand, to silence her. 'But, Miss Trench,' he said very gently, 'you don't want to run a company like Trenco.'

This man is dangerous, Janis thought. He sees too much, too quickly. He makes me see things I hadn't seen before, and I don't like it. She was suddenly convinced that she had to end the discussion, fast. There was no way she could think of making Mr Anson leave before he was ready to. He would hardly be taken in by a faked cry of 'Fire!' So she would have to leave herself, and hope he put it down to female

temper—which it would be. She didn't need to fake
that.

'You have it all wrong!' she snapped back at him.
'You think I'm a silly girl who wants to design
hopelessly impractical dresses, don't you? I don't do
anything like that. I work here, in this office, all day
and every day. Running Trenco. And I intend to keep
on doing it.'

Mr Anson stared at her. 'But why? You don't want
to sell cheap shirts, Miss Trench. You want to be a
designer. That's obvious. That's why you studied for
a fashion diploma, instead of taking a sensible course
in business studies. And can't you see—this is just not
the way to do it.'

'Who on earth are you,' yelled Janis, 'to tell me
what I want? You don't know the first thing about me.
And if I have my way, Mr Anson, you never will!' She
jumped up again, kicking away the typist's chair, and
strode to the door. She stopped for just long enough
to add, 'If you need to know anything else, you can
ask the secretary to tell you,' before she stalked out
through reception, past an enthralled Anthea, and
banged the main door of Trenco Fashions behind her.

She had jerked the handle of her yellow Mini three
times in vain before she remembered that she had left
her car keys in her handbag in the office. There was
no way she was going back to fetch them, not with Mr
Anson still there. She dug her hands into the pockets
of her loose linen jacket, and marched off down the
road.

It was not really a proper road. Trenco Fashions
was on an industrial estate just outside Smithbury. A
maze of service roads wove through the estate, but
there was no through traffic. Nobody ever walked
around the estate, except in the morning and evening,

when the factory workers were making their way to the bus stop on the main road.

Most of the estate units had blank walls fronting on to the service tracks, with just a little high window to mark their reception areas, but Janis still felt uncomfortably conspicuous as she strode along by the side of the road. There was no path, and the ground at the roadside was rough and stony, with patches of nettles and tall grass. She had to hop into some nettles to avoid an impatient rep whizzing around a corner, and she stopped to rub the ankle she had stung through her tights, cursing the car as it disappeared.

She took a look at her watch. Half-past four. Should she walk home? It was nearly two miles, and her high-heeled pumps were not designed for long hikes. Though it was a fine day for February, she still shivered a little: she was dressed for indoors, in a cream linen suit and jade green silk vest, and hadn't expected to walk further than from the main door of Trenco to her car. Nor did she really trust Anthea to lock up the factory behind her, not with Mr Anson there to provide plenty of distraction. She decided she would have to go back, after a few minutes, when she could be reasonably sure he had left.

Just then, a dark blue, open-topped Jaguar drew up by the kerb.

'Can I give you a lift somewhere?' Mr Anson asked.

Janis glowered at him. She was conscious that, however she replied, she was going to look ridiculous. She was still trying to work up a stinging retort when he leaned over and opened the near door of the car from the inside.

'I'll just throw my briefcase in the back,' he said, matching his actions to his words.

Trapped, Janis got in. The car was a vintage

model, with low-slung leather seats which gave beneath her as she settled down.

'The door lock's a little tricky.' He reached over her and pulled it to with a bang. His hand just avoided brushing her thighs, and she smoothed her skirt down self-consciously. 'Were you going into town?'

If she agreed, it would be a three-mile walk home, and she had no money with her for a taxi. She turned to him and gave a sweet smile. 'I'm afraid I'm not going your way at all.'

'No problem, I'm in no hurry,' replied Mr Anson calmly. 'You navigate. Warn me in plenty of time when you want to turn right. I get impatient with women who dither.'

Janis glared again. 'Left at the main road,' she said reluctantly.

The roads were growing busy with rush-hour traffic, and Janis concentrated so hard on giving impeccable directions that she didn't say anything more revealing than 'take the right lane now' or 'left at the traffic lights' until they were nearly at the road where she lived. It struck her, suddenly, that her mother would ask some very embarrassing questions if she looked out of the window and saw Janis arriving home early in Mr Anson's Jaguar.

'It's only just round the corner. I can walk from here.'

'There's nowhere to pull in. Next left?'

'The one after.'

They turned into a broad suburban street, with large redbrick houses set well back in big gardens. Roselea Crescent was precisely the counterpart of Trenco Fashions, as it had been when Janis's father was alive. Solid, prosperous, utterly indifferent to design good or bad, looking as if it would continue

exactly as it was until the end of the world. Janis
pointed out the white gates that gave her mother's
house its name. The paint was peeling slightly, she
noticed for the first time. Her father had intended to
have the house repainted that year but, after his death,
neither she nor her mother had thought to arrange
it.

White Gates. The one solid asset behind Trenco
Fashions. Trenco didn't own its factory; the unit on
the industrial estate was rented. Its only other assets
were a working stock of fabric, thirty-odd sewing
machines, a couple of presses and packing materials.
The company might just be solvent, on paper, putting
book values to all the equipment. But if it came to
receivership, when there would be huge accountants'
bills to pay, when the machines might be sold at
auction for a song—there would never be enough
money to cover the bank loan, let alone pay the folders
full of overdue bills. No, if Mr Anson did advise the
bank to foreclose on their loan—even if he simply
advised them not to lend any more—then the only
solution to the financial crisis would be to sell White
Gates, and pay off the bills with the proceeds.

If only her father had had proper life insurance,
Janis thought to herself, not for the first time, then
everything would have been all right. She could have
taken her time, perhaps brought in a good accountant,
as Mr Anson suggested, slowly set Trenco in order
and moved back to her own design work. But Walter
Trench, like so many self-made businessmen, had
always been too busy to think about that kind of thing,
and Janis's mother had never been the kind of woman
who would think of it for him.

All that added up to a very good reason for being
polite to Mr Anson, however obnoxious he made

himself. After all, he might just dissuade the bank from taking such a drastic step. Janis turned to him as he drew the car to a halt.

'That was very kind of you, Mr Anson.'

'My pleasure.'

'Could I ask you in for a cup of coffee . . .'

The corners of his mouth twitched again. 'Judging by the last cup you made me, I doubt if that would be wise.'

A hot rush of colour flooded over Janis's face. 'My hand must have slipped.'

'Really?'

As Janis reached out to the car door, he stretched out his hand to the ignition, and turned the key towards him. The engine spluttered and died; a horrible silence descended. Janis felt him turn towards her. She twisted round, staring back across the car at him. He had a strong-featured face, with a long nose, a wide mouth and thick, level brows. The dark eyes held hers again, sending a little shiver down her spine.

'Are you are an only child?'

The question surprised her. 'No, I have a younger brother. He's away at university, in Paris. He's studying French—it's his year abroad.'

'So he has nothing to do with Trenco.'

'No, nothing.' Janis hesitated. 'I don't think he ever will. Matthew isn't interested in clothing companies, he wants to be a translator.'

'And does your mother have much to do with the running of the company?'

Janis's eyes opened a shade wider. 'She's a director of Trenco. The only other director, except for Mr Jenkins.'

'So you discuss the business with her? She knows about the cash-flow crisis?'

Janis's hand clenched on the door-handle.

'Are you obliged,' she said carefully, 'to discuss everything you found out today with my co-directors?'

He considered.

'My only obligation, Miss Trench, is to the bank. I just have to report to them, to make sure they are properly informed about the financial situation. That's all I need to do. You're the managing director. If Trenco is operating at a loss, it's your responsibility to discuss it with the rest of the board.'

Janis's hand tightened a little more. Responsibility or not, that was impossible. Mother wasn't that kind of person; it would only panic her to know that there were problems. All right, she'd have to talk to Mr Jenkins, when he had received Mr Anson's report, but she had not even begun to think about how she was going to cope with that, now she had some idea what kind of a report Mr Jenkins was going to get.

'I don't believe we are operating at a loss,' she said defiantly.

'Possibly not. All the same, you could do with some impartial advice. Mr Jenkins is not impartial. His first priority is to protect his investment.'

'Advice,' Janis said sharply, 'tends to come expensive.'

'Mistakes come even more expensive.' He was not looking at her any more, but over her shoulder; and Janis, turning to follow his gaze, saw to her alarm that her mother was coming down the drive.

Mr Anson was already climbing out of the car and, as Janis struggled in vain with the recalcitrant door-lock, he strode around to the pavement and released her. He reached for her hand to pull her out of the low seat and, to her embarrassment, held on to it and gave it a squeeze as her mother reached them.

'Oh, Mother, this is Mr Anson. He's an accountant, who's been doing some work with me this afternoon. My car wouldn't start, and he very kindly gave me a lift home.' She resisted the temptation to glance at him as she delivered this line. 'Mr Anson—my mother, Elizabeth Trench.'

'Marcus, please.' He dropped Janis's hand as he spoke, and reached out to shake her mother's.

Marcus. Yes, it suited him: a solid, Roman sort of a name. Janis felt herself relax a fraction. With Marcus backing up her innocuous tale, she would probably get by without any questions from her mother—except for easily deflected ones about when she was likely to see him again. And she was proud of the way her mother looked. Elizabeth Trench was a conservative dresser, but she was always neat, and her narrowly cut pink dress set off her trim figure, her short grey hair and regular features. She had a tendency to gush over visitors, but that was a welcome distraction just then, and Mr Anson—Marcus—was already explaining that he had a urgent appointment in town, and could not possibly come in.

'You'll—you'll be in touch, then?' Janis met his eyes briefly, but she tried not to make her look seem pleading.

'If there's anything else I need to know. Otherwise, this will all go through the usual channels. So nice to meet you, Mrs Trench.'

Elizabeth Trench watched as the sports car roared off down the road, and disappeared round the corner. 'What a charming young man,' she said. 'But an accountant, dear? Your father never used to talk to accountants, except when he was filling in his tax return.'

That, Janis thought to herself, was the real trouble. She would have managed so much better, taking over Trenco after her father's sudden death, if the company had been in good order. The ledgers had been completely beyond deciphering, though, and the company's auditors never seemed to have made more than a nominal attempt to set them straight.

'Just a routine visit,' she said, as easily as she could. 'Mr Jenkins suggested it. I thought it was a good idea, to make sure I was doing the books properly.'

Her mother gave a little frown, as they moved towards the house. 'I thought your evening class was teaching you all that, Janis.'

'It is, Mother. But slowly.' Janis glanced sideways. The frown was dissipating already. Elizabeth was not a natural worrier: until her husband had died, she had never had anything serious to worry about, and after his death she had offloaded most of the financial concerns on to Janis. Not out of selfishness, not even consciously, Janis suspected. Elizabeth had been so used to her role as a wife who needed to do no more than keep the home tidy and cook the meals, it was difficult for her to take in the fact that, now, going on as she had always done might not be enough.

'I think I might bring the books home, give them a going-over, during the next few weeks. Just so that I have them absolutely right.'

'More work in the evenings? But Janis! You already do so much. If you take on any more, you'll never get out at all in the evenings.'

Janis managed a wry grin. She could hardly explain to her mother how much she hated the prospect of wrestling with the ledgers, while her friends were all out enjoying themselves.' 'That's how it is when you run your own company, Mother,' she said.

'But, Janis, you're twenty-four now, and it isn't as if you have a steady boyfriend. How are you ever going to meet the right man if you don't go out at all? There hasn't been anyone serious since Patrick went off to Italy, has there? And that's over three years ago now. It isn't natural, Janis, not for a lovely girl like you.'

'Oh, Mother! You know how times have changed. There's plenty of time for me to get married and have children. I don't want you worrying yourself over me.'

'But, Janis, I do.' And how inappropriately, Janis could not help thinking, as her mother babbled on, speculating on whether Janis was still pining for Patrick. It was not as if she ever thought of Patrick these days, it had never been more than a college romance, and she had been genuinely glad when he had been offered a marvellous design job with an Italian company. She had been so busy since that there had been no time to look for a boyfriend. It would have been different if one had come her way, but the men who had asked her out had never particularly attracted her. Recently, she had been beginning to think that perhaps she was cut out for a career rather than for marriage and children. Elizabeth Trench would have been horrified to hear her suggest that, though. If Janis was ever to explain, it would have to be when she was more securely established, and when her mother was completely over the shock of being widowed.

'And that young man just now, Janis,' her mother was going on. 'He was obviously really keen, bringing you all the way home like that, and you hardly gave him a sideways glance. An accountant, too. You should have encouraged him a little, Janis. I'm sure he would have come in if you'd pressed him, then . . . who knows what would have happened?'

Most likely, Janis thought to herself, he would have dropped heavy hints about Trenco's financial crisis. 'Oh, Mother,' she repeated, 'he was just being polite. He's probably married, anyway.'

'I saw the way he took your hand,' her mother persisted. 'And he did say he would be in touch with you again.'

'Only over business.'

'Well, why don't you invite him here, and discuss your business over dinner? After all, I am a director of Trenco, aren't I, darling?'

'And a very important one, Mother,' Janis assured her. 'I'll certainly think about it, if I need to see him again.'

It was strange, being home so early. Janis usually dashed into the house at a quarter to six, ready for dinner at six, and often dashed out again afterwards, back to the factory. It flustered her mother a little, she could see, that she should have come home before dinner was all ready. She murmured something about telephoning a garage, and retreated upstairs to her studio, leaving her mother to potter peacefully around the kitchen.

The studio was cold. She had hardly worked there at all that winter, hardly even been up there, and it had the chilly-walled feel of a room where no heating has been on for week after week of cold weather. She climbed on to the old kitchen table she used to spread out her drawings, and reached up to open the high dormer window.

The late afternoon sun streamed in. Like all of White Gates, the studio was spotlessly clean. Elizabeth swept and dusted it twice a week. It looked unused, though. The drawings pinned to the walls were ones Janis had finished the year before; her easel had no paper fixed on it, and last year's indian ink was solidifying in its plastic bottles. Janis had spent so much time there, in the years at college, and during those first glorious few months at Trenco, when she had been working on designs to show to the chain-store buyers.

She had got as far as making up the first prototypes of her loose tops and shirtdresses—and then had come the terrible car crash, and the days when she and her mother had haunted the hospital, waiting for her father to die. After the funeral, she had bundled all the prototypes into a box which she shoved to the back of the factory store room, and taken over her father's desk. She had thought, at first, that she might be able to get back to work on them after a couple of weeks. But the problems had multiplied, the bills and the suppliers and the women in the factory all demanded so much of her time, and the couple of weeks had turned into a year.

A year in which Trenco, starved of the change of direction she and her father had planned, had floundered along, producing old-fashioned shirts to meet smaller and smaller orders from its regular customers. A year in which Janis's designs had become out of date. They were last year's colours, with last year's detail. She would have to start again, if she ever did manage to turn her ideas into real garments on shop rails.

Manage? Managing seemed more and more impossible, just then. She hadn't the time or the money to finish making the transition that her father had planned, even on a small scale; and if she carried on with Trenco as it had been, it looked all too likely that she would end up presiding over the company's collapse. She was running as hard as she could, all the time, and still going backwards.

'Janis!' her mother called, from the foot of the stairs. 'Dinner!'

Six o'clock exactly. At least Elizabeth Trench's little domain ran as smoothly as ever. Two small glasses of cream sherry would be ready poured, the table spread with embroidered linen and set with silver, the dinner perfectly cooked. 'Coming,' Janis called, and ran down the stairs, trying to think up a convincing tale about her car.

After supper was over and the washing up put away, Janis excused herself and left the house. Her mother was already installed in front of the television, watching one of the soap operas she followed so avidly.

Really, I'm not much company for Mother, Janis thought to herself as she set out on the long walk back to Trenco and her handbag. The only one left at home with her now, and I hardly see her, except at meal times. She's always cheerful about it, but she must get desperately lonely. Too lonely, Janis knew, for her yet to think seriously of leaving home. Those meal times were little enough, but they meant so much to her mother.

Twenty-four had never been Janis's deadline for getting married, but it was the age when she had expected to move into a flat of her own, and now she seemed further away from it than ever. Unless White Gates did have to be sold, she thought sadly, then she and her mother might end up in a flat together.

A week ago, Janis would have found the idea unthinkable. Somehow, though, Marcus Anson's warnings had kicked away the block in her own mind that had kept her from seeing how badly things were going. She could see it all too clearly, now. She simply had no idea how she was going to rescue the situation.

Certainly, Marcus Anson would be no help. The one thing Janis needed most was time: the time that would enable her to keep Trenco going until she managed somehow to produce some new designs, and set the company firmly in its new direction. But time had to be bought, with money from the bank, and Marcus Anson clearly was not going to advise the bank to buy it. No, he would tell Mr Jenkins that Trenco had become a bad risk.

It was so unfair! Janis couldn't help thinking to herself. Nobody had warned her. Mr Graham, who did Trenco's auditing, had occasionally murmured that the books were less than perfect, but he'd never pressed her father to improve them, never seemed to see any problems lingering under their impenetrable entries. If the bank had sent another man like Mr Graham, she might have been given a dose of friendly sympathy and advice; but instead Marcus Anson had blown through her office like a whirlwind, and devastated all her efforts.

Janis turned into the estate, and made her way slowly through the deserted factory buildings. Her Mini was the only car on the parking area in front of the smart red Trenco sign. She tried the factory door, was reassured to find that Anthea had indeed locked up, let herself in with the spare key, and walked through to her office.

The ledgers were still piled up on her desk. Janis went to sit behind it, on the chair Marcus Anson had used that afternoon. She glanced around, seeing the office as he must have seen it. The shabby desks, scuffed and scratched from years of hard use. The

worn cord carpet, the battered filing cabinets, with
their drawers bulging open and leaking folders of
unpaid bills. Anthea's row of geraniums on the high
windowsill, lovingly tended and watered; her own
avocado plants and tiny orange trees, lining the
frosted glass partition that separated the office from
the factory workroom. A calendar from the Chinese
take-away on the main road. Fashion drawings she
had done at college and in her first job for a big
clothing company, and a set of Cézanne prints,
pinned up edge to edge to cover the expanse of dirty
cream paint. It was scruffy, she supposed, but it was
hers. Hers, somehow, in a way that White Gates never
could be. Sell Trenco? Never, never, never!

On her desk, next to the ledgers, there was a phone
pad, and the top sheet of paper was covered with notes
in an unfamiliar, strongly angular hand. Janis tore it
off, and glanced at them. 'Manual d/e?? PC? PC.' The
second 'PC' was underlined, and Janis frowned. Who
was 'PC'? The sharp young banker who would close
down Trenco, to make sure his bank got their money
back? And to hell with thirty machinists, Anthea, her
mother and herself! Janis slammed her hand on the
desk, crumpled the piece of paper, and shoved it
angrily in the bin.

She had no stomach for working just then. Instead,
she took the Mini down to the coast, driving out
through the town to the cliff road. It was growing
dark when she stopped the car and strode off, across
the rough grass to the edge of the cliff. She walked
along the clifftop for maybe two miles; slowly, into
the wind, as she went away from the car, and then
faster, with it pushing behind her, moulding her coat
to her legs and blowing her hair into her eyes, on her
way back.

The walk did not calm her. She had an uncomfortably strong memory of Marcus Anson's dark, disconcerting gaze, of the touch of his hand as he had squeezed hers outside White Gates. Had he meant to threaten her, she wondered? Or to reassure her? Somehow, by coming into her office, prying through her ledgers, seeing the house where she lived, he seemed to have invaded her privacy, taken away all her self-reliance. She shook out her windblown hair as she settled back into the car, feeling thankful that she would have no cause to see him again.

CHAPTER TWO

JANIS looked in the mirror over her dressing-table. She gave a little frown, and then turned it into a smile. She combed her hair again, applied a touch more lipstick, and smeared a hint of brown eyeshadow on her lids. She smiled again, more confidently.

She was dressed for her interview with Mr Jenkins at the bank, and the brown woollen skirt and deep red jumper had been chosen to reassure him. They brought out the highlights in her short chestnut hair, and emphasised the paleness of her skin. She needed to look smart, without being aggressively fashionable; to look like a factory owner, not a secretary dressing to please her boss. Her only frivolous touch was the pair of very high-heeled red shoes she slipped on. She was a little taller than Mr Jenkins, even in flat shoes; wearing these, she thought with a touch of amusement, she would tower over him.

In her car, she kicked off the red shoes, and slipped on a pair of flat-soled pumps. The Mini's clutch was temperamental, and she always felt unsafe driving in heeled shoes. Then she waved goodbye to her mother —who had no idea she was going to the bank, and not to the factory—and set off for town.

It was always difficult, parking in the centre of Smithbury, even out of season, and Janis had left plenty of time. But a two-hour parking space presented itself just along the road from the bank, so she sneaked the car in neatly, yanked on the handbrake, and grabbed her briefcase before locking up.

She was in a wide street just off Eastbourne Road, the main shopping street. It was full of estate agents' and building society offices. Janis glanced along at the plate glass windows, and at the little plaques by the side doors, announcing the inhabitants of the offices above. 'Jones and Jones, Solicitors and Commissioners for Oaths'. 'Anson and Williams, Accountants'.

Her eyes moved on, and then something clicked in her head, and they moved back again. Anson and Williams. That, surely, was Marcus Anson's firm. Was he, she wondered, a junior member of the family firm? Or was he the Anson on the plaque? It was disconcerting to see the name so unexpectedly. Though it was hardly surprising, Janis reminded herself firmly, that Mr Jenkins should have used a firm of accountants just down the road from his own bank.

Janis checked her watch, then drifted into Eastbourne Road. Her appointment with Mr Jenkins was in fifteen minutes, but she knew he always overran his appointments, so it would not do to be too early. She glanced at the windows of the chain stores, taking in the spring colours and designs. There was a lot of strident cerise, and of banana yellow.

Janis cared deeply about colour, which she felt sold more clothes than did the cut of the garment. It annoyed her that cloth manufacturers tended to be so limited in their outlook. If one large firm murmured 'banana yellow' in their ears, they would flood the whole market with banana yellow, and woe betide anyone who had hoped to buy pale primrose instead. The only way to get hold of an unusual or unfashionable shade was to give a firm an enormous order, or to dye your own cloth—and Janis did not have the resources to do that.

That banana yellow would blend well with gauloise blue, she was thinking as she turned back towards the bank. It would still be fashionable, but more easily wearable than the cerise combination. Not that it was any use planning banana-yellow garments. She had to compete with sketches in the design rooms, not with clothes already on the racks and, by the time her own clothes were in production, a new colour would have stolen the limelight.

Mr Jenkins was still busy when she reached the bank, and she slipped into one of the low chairs in the waiting area. Immediately, she felt nervous. 'PC', she thought again, uneasily. It had struck her the night after Marcus Anson's visit that 'PC' might stand for 'Police Constable'. That was two weeks previously, and during every evening of those two weeks she had worked through the audited accounts. They had not yet yielded up all their mysteries, but Janis was as sure as she could be that her father had never done anything remotely illegal.

She thought of going over the figures in her briefcase again, and promptly decided against it. She knew them all as well as she could hope to in the circumstances, and she had a feeling that Marcus Anson would have summarised them more efficiently than she ever could. Instead, she fished out her sketch pad. It might calm her, she thought, to make a note of the ideas that had been drifting through her head as she checked out the shop windows. A flared skirt to complement the new, thinner line of blouse, with a hemline just above the knee? Or just below? She doodled and sketched alternative ideas on the pad until Mr Jenkins's secretary called her in.

Janis had known Mr Jenkins, short and dapper, since she was a child. That was not necessarily an advantage, she knew. She sometimes felt that he found it hard to make the transition from seeing her as her father's little girl into treating her as an adult customer. If she had not inherited the bank loan together with Trenco, she might have been tempted to switch to a different bank, where the manager would look at her with fresh eyes. Mr Jenkins was well-intentioned, though, and whatever Marcus Anson had suggested Janis believed he would not ditch his long-standing customers unless there really was no alternative.

The phone rang almost before she was seated, and she glanced across Mr Jenkins's desk as he took the call. Piles of buff client files on the corners. An executive-style desk tidy, the kind family men get for Christmas, with a space for paperclips, one for rubber bands and another for a family snapshot. And, in the large, empty expanse in the middle of the desk, a report. Several pages from the look of it, in a clear-fronted folder, through which she could see the top sheet. It was headed 'Anson and Williams'. The report was pointed towards Mr Jenkins and, from upside-down, without peering too obviously, she could only read the letterhead. That was printed in a modern typeface, in a strong, bright blue. Not the family firm, she decided.

'Do forgive me, Janis. Problems, problems. Can't get away from them.' Mr Jenkins gave her an avuncular smile. 'And how is your charming mother?'

Janis poured out the usual platitudes, and they went on to discuss her brother, Mr Jenkins's wife, and his daughter Marie, who was newly married with a first grandchild on the way. Janis felt her foot begin to tap impatiently under the desk, and she deliberately stilled it. There were many advantages, she reminded herself, to doing business in the old-fashioned, personal way.

Before he had so much as glanced at the report, the secretary popped in to remind Mr Jenkins that his next client was waiting. He greeted this news with easy surprise, and then, when the secretary closed the door again, his manner changed ever so slightly. He picked up the report, let his eyes drift over the first page, and flicked through the rest of it.

'It seems you have a few little problems, Janis.'

No, lots of big problems and one enormous one, Janis thought to herself. The whopper being Marcus Anson and his opinion of Trenco.

'I've had difficulty finding time to get the books straight,' she admitted. 'But I realise now how essential it is, and I've set about it in earnest already. By the end of the month, I should be in a position to give you some financial forecasts. I'm hoping you'll agree to be patient till then, and to increase our overdraft facility just a little in the meantime, to tide us over this temporary crisis.'

'Ever prepared a financial forecast, Janis?'

'Well, not exactly. But I've been learning about them at my evening classes.'

There was a short silence. Mr Jenkins drank a gulp of his coffee.

'Anson has some very interesting suggestions here,' he said.

I know exactly what they are, Janis thought glumly to herself.

'I've thought very hard about it, Mr Jenkins,' she said. 'And I would be prepared to try to find an outside investor in the company, so that in the long run we can repay some of the bank finance. I have an uncle who might help. But I really am not interested in winding up the company, unless there is absolutely no alternative.'

'Winding it up! Whatever gave you that idea?'

Janis decided it would be unwise to reveal where that idea had come from. 'It was just a . . .' her voice trailed off.

'No, what you need is a decent financial system, one that will help you keep on top of your creditors and avoid this kind of crisis again. You could certainly use a little more working capital, but there's no need to look for major new investors until you're ready to expand. It's how the bank makes its money, backing businesses like yours. The last thing we want is for you to replace us.' Mr Jenkins gave a broad smile at this point, and Janis managed a wavery one in return. 'So, my feeling is,' he continued, 'that we should agree to put Anson's recommendations into operation, and then give it a year or so to see how things turn out.'

So Marcus Anson had not recommended the bank to foreclose on their loan; he had deliberately misled Janis. There she was, all ready to face the end of Trenco, and instead he had recommended—what on earth *had* he recommended?

'I'm afraid Mr Anson didn't tell me what he was going to recommend to you, Mr Jenkins.'

'Oh, forgive me, my dear! I was thinking that the two of you had obviously got on so well that there was no need to explain. But, of course, Anson would never reveal his recommendations directly to anyone but his client. Look, why don't you read his report? There are a few other things he mentioned to me face to face, but the gist of it all is there.'

Woodenly, Janis accepted the plastic folder. She had to read through the report twice before any of the words sank in. There were the expected remarks about the terrible ledgers, couched this time in more diplomatic language. Recommendations that Trenco set up a computer-based accounting system, which could be run by a competent clerk once it was properly established. Some comments on cash-flow forecasting, which meant less to her than she would have been prepared to admit. Calculations of the amount of money Trenco would need to borrow to survive the crisis, and how soon it might be repaid. And . . .

'So, what it comes down to,' she said slowly, 'is that we should invite Mr Graham to join the board as our accounting advisor.'

'Mr Graham? Oh no, my dear! Jim Graham may be a pleasant chap, but he's hardly a whiz with these new-fangled PCs. No, the idea was that Anson should join you, as a second bank nominee to the board. It was in our agreement with your father that we could nominate two board members if we chose, and this is obviously the time to do it, when we're increasing your loan. Anson reckons he can spare a couple of days a week for the next few months, till the systems are properly in order, and then he'll be on call to advise you and keep a proper eye on things after that.'

The report fluttered, unheeded, from Janis's hand, and landed with a little plop on the edge of Mr Jenkins's desk. Her face went white.

'*Marcus Anson.* On the board of Trenco?'

'It really is a godsend, isn't it, my dear? The perfect arrangement. I must admit, I was just a little worried about how you were going to cope with the company after your father died, but with Anson to keep tabs on you I'll know I can sleep soundly at nights.'

That's a lot more than I will do, Janis thought, appalled. She tried in vain to think of an acceptable

way of protesting, but Mr Jenkins was already rising
from his chair, and dropping her file into his 'OUT'
tray.

'I thought we might have lunch together, maybe
next week,' he said cheerfully as he showed her to the
door. 'Just you and I and Anson, to start things off on
the right foot. And your mother, of course. The new
board of Trenco! Have a word with my secretary, and
let her know when you'll be free. You'll want to write
formally to Anson, of course, as company secretary,
inviting him to join you. And you'll need to add his
name to your letterhead. Can't think of anything else
right now. Anson will know what the formalities are.
He'll be able to tell you just what he had in mind.'

He certainly will do that, Janis thought as she
stumbled down the stairs and collapsed in the front
seat of her yellow Mini. The little bronze plaque with
'Anson and Williams' on it glared at her through the
car window. She had a terrible temptation to rush up
the stairs next to it, and hurl her briefcase full of
papers at Marcus Anson. Instead, she started the car,
and drove, very carefully, back to the factory.

By the time she reached the factory, Janis's initial fury
had died down. Marcus Anson hadn't deliberately
duped her, she decided; he could hardly have told her
he had changed his mind about Trenco, or warned her
what his recommendations would be. But why had he
done it? What did an accountant like Marcus Anson
want with a company like Trenco? She had seen his
figures, and knew that the fee he had proposed for his
two days a week was on the low side, by accountants'
standards. Unless he was really short of work, he
would hardly be doing it for the money, and she
couldn't for the life of her see how else he might gain.

She hadn't many influential friends she could recommend him to, and by the bank's standards Trenco was small beer, so he'd not win exceptional gratitude from Mr Jenkins. It was a mystery, and it worried her.

She phoned him herself. It would be better, she thought, than leaving him to phone her and take her unawares. She was cowardly enough to wait until Anthea had gone on a swift errand to the baker's. The deep voice at the other end of the line was polite and impersonal. He called her 'Miss Trench', went succinctly through all the steps she would need to take to bring him on to the board, and arranged to come into the factory the following afternoon.

It might not be so bad, she thought. At least it was some kind of an answer to her troubles, at a time when she hadn't expected to find any answer to all. She wrote out a formal letter to him, and a second to Companies House, and left them by Anthea's desk for typing. She wanted Marcus Anson's arrival to seem perfectly routine, the kind of thing that hardly merited a special word with Anthea. However, they would have to rearrange the office, she supposed, buy him a desk and chair and whatever else he needed, even his own coffee mug. It was a pity there was only one office. It might be possible to fix up a second one, by partitioning off part of the reception area, but she did not dare to plan to spend extra money on that unless he suggested it himself.

The state of the ledgers had improved in the last two weeks, Janis knew, thanks to her hard work in the evenings, but she still had a feeling that Marcus Anson would find plenty to complain about. She was in no mood to face his complaints, so she launched into a blitz on the overdue accounts, churning out statements and making telephone calls to the worst offenders.

Anthea reappeared with two rather greasy paper bags. 'Apple and cinnamon for you,' she announced cheerily, dumping one on Janis's desk, 'and raspberry jam for me.'

She sat down, ripped her bag open, and took a large bite of its contents. Then she froze, as she caught sight of Janis's letter.

'Mr Anson!' she squealed, when she had swallowed the doughnut. 'Janis Trench, do you mean to tell me that you've hired that gorgeous man who was here the other day?'

'I haven't exactly hired him,' Janis said. 'It's more that he's hired himself.'

'You mean he'll be coming to work here? With us?'

'He will. Part time,' Janis added, disparagingly.

'No more doughnuts, then.' Anthea wrapped the torn bag around the rest of her snack, and lobbed it in the wastebin. Janis watched her, amazed. 'I mean,' Anthea went on, 'they do stick to the hips, don't they?'

'I shouldn't think Mr Anson will notice.'

'No, but I will. When's he coming? *Tomorrow?* Heavens, I won't lose many pounds by then.'

'You haven't gained many pounds since he last saw you,' Janis said. Involuntarily, her eyes narrowed as she sized up her secretary. A divorcee in her late twenties, Anthea fizzed and bubbled so much that nobody ever seemed to notice her size-fourteen-and-a-bit hips.

'Maybe he likes his ladies cuddly,' Anthea went on cheerfully. Then, belatedly, she seemed to realise that Janis's reaction was rather different from her own. 'You are pleased, aren't you, Janis? It's what we need around here, a man, isn't it? I mean, there hasn't been a man in the place . . . well, for ages.'

Since her father had died. And Janis could remember only too well how all the women in the factory had fussed over her father, giggled and blushed whenever he came into the workshop to talk to them. She could just imagine the stir Marcus Anson would cause. Especially . . .

'Maybe,' she said coldly, 'he's married.'

Anthea gave her a mischievous smile. 'Maybe he's fallen for you.'

Oh, no, Janis told herself. He had definitely, definitely not fallen for her.

'And now,' Elizabeth Trench said, 'Janis will be free to get on with her designing, won't she, Mr Anson? Marcus,' she corrected herself with a smile. 'It's what her father always intended, you know—for Janis to be Trenco's designer.'

'That isn't the idea at all, Mother,' Janis broke in hurriedly. 'Mr Anson is only working temporarily on the books, just till the new system is established. Then I'll be running Trenco again myself.'

She avoided Marcus Anson's eyes as she spoke, and smiled brightly at her mother. Her mother seemed to be thoroughly enjoying the business lunch, though it had been an ordeal for Janis. She was acutely conscious of Marcus Anson sitting next to her, and of every movement he made. There seemed to be a charge of electricity running between the two of them, as if any move which brought them too close would weld them together irresistibly. Every time she had glanced at him, his dark eyes had connected with hers, sending currents of alarm pulsing through her body. Even the sound of his deep voice gave her a thrill of awareness.

'Marcus,' he said into her ear, in a gentle reminder that she was the only one who persisted in calling him 'Mr Anson'. She even called him that in the office, though to Anthea he was already Marcus. 'I'm afraid Janis is quite right, Mrs Trench. This isn't the time for Trenco to change direction. We need to establish the firm on a solid footing again before we think of making any changes. And, fortunately, there seems to be plenty of work at the moment.'

We! Janis bridled at that. Marcus Anson was too fond of that word.

Just having him in the office, with his big desk and his shiny new PC—his personal computer, of course—would not have been so bad. He was friendly, house-trained—though he never condescended to make the coffee—got on well with Anthea without flirting with her too unbearably. It was what he was doing that ruffled Janis. Admittedly, he had every right to design the accounting systems exactly as he chose; but he was doing so much more than that. He pronounced his opinions on Trenco's policy. He had vetoed several of Janis's own ideas about the contracts they should accept and the stocks they should buy in; and he had thrust his own ideas at her, right from the first day. He seemed to think he was a part of Trenco, while to Janis he was very definitely an outsider who had been foisted on to *her* company.

Maybe Janis had once let herself think that it would be a relief to sell Trenco, and go back to her design-ing. But, faced with this contest for control, she had swiftly come to the conclusion that she would never be able to bear letting the company fall into the hands of Marcus Anson.

She glanced around at her mother and Mr Jenkins,

but they were both smiling indulgently. They both thoroughly approved, she thought furiously, of this takeover bid. They both backed up everything Marcus Anson said or suggested. If she dared to disagree with him, if she dared to fight for her own company, then she found herself completely out in the cold, with everyone gazing in sorrowful amazement at her. Except for Marcus Anson. His typical expression when he looked at her was one of cool amusement.

Her only consolation was that he could not possibly know of her physical attraction to him. Unlike Anthea, she had always treated him coldly and formally, and he had responded in kind. There had been no more lifts home, and this was only the second time he and her mother had met.

'Of course,' she said, 'there are some long-term problems connected with the shirt contracts. I'm hoping to phase over slowly into producing some more original designs.'

A firm kick on the ankle made her jump, and she covered the movement as well as she could with a little shuffle on her chair.

'But, though the books need a bit of attention,' Marcus Anson said smoothly, 'basically, Trenco seems to be in a reasonable shape.'

'It won't be if . . .'

The kick this time was harder, and Marcus cut in firmly, saying to her mother, 'Your husband built up a remarkably strong workforce, Mrs Trench.'

'Didn't he . . .' Elizabeth Trench burbled on about Marianne and Stella and Joan and the rest of the machinists at Trenco. Janis, pinned between her and Marcus, seethed with annoyance at her blindness.

Mr Jenkins was not quite so blind. 'Don't you

worry, Janis,' he said, when Elizabeth had finished her exposition. 'Marcus will let you know as soon as you're in a position to take a few little risks. And only little ones, mind you. None of this way-out stuff, not while we're backing you.'

'More coffee?' Marcus said, distracting her before she had a chance to bridle at this. He reached for the pot the waitress had left on the table. His free hand just touched the bare skin of her arm as he poured the coffee carefully into her cup. When he moved across to fill her mother's cup, she could feel the imprint his fingers had left behind, burning into her as if he had branded her. Marking her for his, as casually and completely as he had marked her company. And as superficially. Marcus Anson did not have any feelings, of that she was certain. He was the classic bachelor, using his charm and his physical appeal to win women over, but offering them nothing more personal once they had succumbed.

'I should be getting back,' Janis said abruptly, pushing away the cup. 'I have a buyer coming this afternoon, and I want to be in good time to see her.'

'You do have time to give me a lift home first, Janis?' her mother reminded her.

Janis hesitated. She had forgotten that her mother's car was in the garage for a service, and that she had collected her herself and brought her into town. 'If we set off right away,' she said.

'Why don't you leave your mother your car, Janis?' Marcus said. 'I wanted to come over to the factory this afternoon, so I can take you there, and then drop you back home afterwards.'

Janis glared at him. It was the last thing she wanted, to leave with Marcus. To drive back to Trenco with Marcus. To have Marcus intervening in her meeting

with the buyer, making all the decisions, quietly
triumphant when he knew he had negotiated better
terms than she would have settled for. 'How kind,'
she said in a voice packed with venom.

Mr Jenkins winked at her as they said their
goodbyes. Did he imagine, Janis thought furiously,
that Marcus's gesture was any more than a ploy to
appease her mother? It would be the last straw, if Mr
Jenkins believed she was under Marcus's spell. She
stalked out of the door of the restaurant, preferring to
seem ill-mannered rather than to give the impression
of enjoying Marcus's attention.

'It's the green MG,' he said, pointing out his car.

'You've sold the Jaguar?'

'No, but it's minus a distributor at the moment.' He
glanced at her. 'It's one of my hobbies, renovating old
sports cars of the fifties and sixties. I buy them
cheaply at auctions, and keep them in a garage out by
Southtown Road. I usually have three or four at a
time, and I drive them all, pretty much at random—so
long as all the vital components are in place.'

'That figures,' Janis said.

'What does?'

She shrugged. 'They suit you.'

Marcus grinned. 'Let me finish for you. You think
of them as aggressive, showy, petrol-hungry beasts,
all shiny paintwork and shabby leather interiors.
Wonderful to look at, hell to drive, and prone to
unexpected failures at the wrong moment.'

Janis laughed, in spite of herself. It was so exactly
what she had been thinking, and hadn't dared to say.

'Like to drive it?' he asked, surprisingly, offering
her the keys.

Janis shook her head, and slipped into the low,
lumpy seat. Marcus turned to look at her as he slid

behind the wheel, and for a moment their eyes locked. It gave her a curious sensation of intimacy, and for a split second she almost expected him to lean across and kiss her. Then the spell was broken as suddenly as it had descended, and the MG's half-restored engine roared unevenly into life.

'What do you do in your spare time?' he asked companionably.

'What spare time?' The bitter remark came out before she could stop it. She covered it, quickly. 'I've always liked singing. I was in the school choir, and when I left school I joined the local Bach Society. And I swim regularly, and play tennis in the summer.'

'You swim at the local baths?'

'Yes, of course.'

'I've always preferred the sea.' He smiled across at her. 'That's probably why we've never crossed paths.'

'We've probably been to the same places several times without even noticing each other. Smithbury's a small town.'

It was a lie. She would have noticed him anywhere, any time. He gave her another glance, that seemed to say that he knew it was a lie, and then fell silent.

It was some time before Janis realised that he had turned off the road to the industrial estate, and was making for the coast.

'Hey!' she said, alarmed. 'I have to get back to meet the buyer.'

'Your appointment is for three-thirty,' Marcus said, swinging off the main coast road on to a narrow track that led to the cliffs. 'I phoned in and checked with Anthea this morning. And it's only half-past two. I'll get you back with time to spare.'

'What on earth do you have in mind?'

'A talk,' he said, as the MG squealed to a halt on the

rough gravel of the little cliff car park. 'What else?'

'I have absolutely nothing to say to you, Marcus Anson, that I can't say in the office.'

'But I,' he replied, 'have plenty to say to you.' He pocketed the keys and clambered out of the car, walking round to her side. Janis did not move, and he opened the car door, then reached down to take her arm and pull her out and towards him. The pleasant man who had chatted in the car had gone; this was a different animal, and a much more dangerous one. They stood perhaps six inches apart, with Marcus's hard grip on her upper arms maintaining the distance precisely.

'You are not so bloody stupid, Janis Trench, that you don't know that Trenco is in dire trouble at the moment. Not the little cash-flow problem that Jenkins imagines we have. Half the contracts you've been taking on don't even cover your running expenses. We have to turn this company around, and fast, before we present the figures to Jenkins and your mother at the year end. And, instead of backing me up in what I tell them, you go and contradict me, right, left and centre. Well, you can damn well stop acting like a spoilt child, and start supporting me for a change!'

Janis struggled to free her arms and, finding them securely pinned by Marcus's strong hands, lashed out with her foot instead. Marcus, taken by surprise when her shoe connected with his calf, loosed his grip; and Janis's hand was half-way to his cheek before he caught it again.

'*Our* company!' she shouted at him. '*We* have to do this, *we* have to do that! I'll have you know, Marcus Anson, this is *my* company! *I* run Trenco. And I'm not having any damned hired hand tell me what to do with it.'

Marcus's dark eyes blazed, and his mouth thinned into an angry line. His hands pinned hers in an iron grip; she was trapped between him and the car.

'Right now,' he said tightly, 'Trenco belongs to the bank. They can close down the whole operation at a moment's notice. And, if anything happens to shake Jenkins's confidence in the job *we* are doing, he will do just that. Don't kid yourself that Jenkins is a friendly uncle figure who'll pat your hand and lend you another few thousand to see you through. He's a cowardly, conservative banker who can't see an inch beyond the current bottom line. If he believes his money is seriously at risk, he will call in every last penny. Oh, he might cry crocodile tears all the way to the bailiff's, but he won't save you, my girl. Or your empty-headed mother.'

'And you will?' she scoffed.

'I'll have a damned good try!'

Janis glared back at him, detesting him with every inch of her being; and then something in his expression made her relax a fraction. It was true, she reminded herself, he *was* trying. He had worked efficiently and unrelentingly, till long after six, on each of the days he had come to the factory.

The iron hands eased and then released her, and she rubbed her wrists where his fingers had imprinted them with angry red marks.

'I don't understand,' she said quietly. 'What's in this for you? You don't own shares in Trenco. If we do recover, you'll not make any profit out of us.' She hesitated. 'Or will you? Have you done some kind of a deal with Jenkins? A block of the bank's shares as soon as we go into the black? A profit-sharing arrangement? Or were you hoping to buy your way into my mother's favour?'

'At least,' he said contemptuously, 'you don't imagine I'm trying to con your own shares away from you.'

'I wouldn't put it past you.'

'You stupid idiot! You say one more thing like that to me, and you'll get my resignation in return. And then you can see how kindly Jenkins will treat you.' He pushed her angrily away from the car door, and opened it. 'Get in. We'll be late.'

Janis had not moved. 'I'm not playing it like that,' she persisted. 'You and me against my mother and Mr Jenkins? Plotting together, keeping them in the dark. It's no way to run a company.'

'Would you rather we called your mother in and went through the figures with her? How do you think she would react, if she knew you were on the verge of bankruptcy? That there was a good chance she'd lose every penny she possessed, and her house into the bargain? Whose side do you think she would take?'

Janis did not answer. She pushed past him, and sat, rigidly, in the car. Marcus returned to the driver's side.

They drove in silence until they reached the factory. Janis's mind was racing, alarmed, confused, desperately disturbed by the scene on the cliff. When Marcus stopped the car outside the factory, she turned to him again.

'You misled Jenkins, didn't you? In your report on the company?'

He swung round angrily towards her, and then paused before he replied. 'Not in the way you're suggesting. My report was one hundred per cent accurate. Jenkins might disagree with some of my interpretations, but there's nothing in the figures I gave him that he could question. And, if I didn't believe I could pull Trenco round and make a profit for the bank, I wouldn't have advised him to back you any further. I've done nothing unethical, if that's what you're suggesting. But there are figures I've uncovered since that I don't want Jenkins to see at this stage. If he did, he might override my judgement and react instantly. That would be painful for you. And it would be painful for me, too, if that's what you want to know.'

'So you couldn't back out now, if you wanted to.'

'Right now? Sure, I could. I'd lose some face, but it's not been long, and I could persuade Jenkins that I'd discovered the vital figures after today's lunch, and not before. But from now onwards we get into this deeper, both of us. For maybe six months, we keep Jenkins and your mother at arm's length. If you tell them too much, we'll most likely both go down. Both of us together.'

It was an unnerving confession. For reasons she did not pretend to comprehend, Marcus Anson had chosen to put himself at her mercy. He might be planning to mislead Mr Jenkins and her mother, but with her, it seemed, he had chosen to be bluntly, disconcertingly honest.

'You want promises from me?' Janis asked slowly.

Marcus shook his head. 'I'd prefer your trust. There's no need to promise anything. But I must have your co-operation. We'll never succeed otherwise. And, for a start, I sit in on your negotiations with the buyer this afternoon.'

'You win.' That one you win, Janis added to herself. But, if you try to change my company in ways I can't accept, Marcus Anson, then I will fight you. Every inch of the way, even if we both go under in the process!

CHAPTER THREE

'MISS TRENCH?'

Janis looked up from her desk to see one of her machinists poking her head around the office door.

'Yes, Stella?'

'Could I have a word with you, Miss Trench? In private?'

'Of course you can, Stella.' Janis glanced across the office. Marcus was buried in his computer, and Anthea was typing invoices. 'I'll be in the storeroom, Anthea, if anybody phones for me.'

She and Stella walked through the workroom together, past the rows of women with their sewing machines buzzing away, past the steaming presses, and into the little storeroom at the end of the factory. It was immaculately neat, with bales of poly-cotton shirting, flat piles of empty cardboard boxes, and stacks of finished shirts, all folded, wrapped in cellophane, and labelled ready for shipping.

Janis sat down on a little stool that was used for reaching to the higher shelves, and motioned Stella to squat on the bottom rung of the stepladder. 'Was it a personal problem, Stella?'

It had always been her father's style to encourage all his employees to confide in him. And, if they did have **problems, Janis knew that he had often done a little** extra to help them, finding them overtime when it wasn't strictly necessary, or giving them time off to see to sick children. She didn't want to change these practices, but at the same time she was painfully conscious that there was little scope for generosity while Trenco was in difficulties.

'It's my Bill, Miss Trench. You know, he was a maintenance man down at the yard.'

The little shipyard in Smithbury had just cut its workforce in half, blaming economic problems and falling orders.

'He's lost his job?'

Stella nodded miserably. She was a thin woman in her late thirties, with wispy brown hair and dark circles under her eyes. 'Course, he's looking around, Miss Trench, but you know what it's like, with so many men and so few jobs going. And—well, the thing that really worried us was, there was a rumour that, with Mr Anson coming in, it was a sign that Trenco wasn't doing so well either.'

Janis forced a smile. 'It's not the way a firm folds up, Stella, by bringing in a top accountant. We're restructuring things a little, but that's so we can plan for expansion.' Stella looked doubtful, and Janis stumbled on. 'You know we've got plenty of orders at the moment. And, though I wouldn't want to raise your hopes too high, there's a chance there will be some overtime going in the summer, if the buyers show any interest in my new designs.'

'You're going to produce your own designs, Miss Trench?'

'Well, I'm hoping,' said Janis, hoping mainly at that moment that what she was saying would not get back to Marcus Anson. 'Though we'll be doing mostly shirts for the time being.'

Stella smiled back, wanly. 'That's good news, miss. I don't suppose you'd be looking for a maintenance man yourself? For the factory?'

Janis shook her head. 'I'm sorry, Stella, but we rely on the estate management for maintenance services. Though I could mention your Bill to them, in case they have any vacancies coming up.'

'I'd be ever so grateful, Miss Trench.'

'My pleasure, Stella. I promise you, there's nothing to worry about here.'

When Janis got back to the office, Marcus looked up and caught her glance. He swung round, very deliberately, away from the video screen.

'Anything wrong?'

'Personal problems,' Janis said tersely. Marcus looked worried. 'Stella's, not mine,' she added.

Marcus recognised the brush-off. He held her look for a moment more, and then he turned back to his work.

But they *were* her problems, Janis knew, even if at second hand. It was her problem that she had been trapped into telling Stella white lies, her problem that thirty-odd employees were relying upon her to keep Trenco going. It was she who had to keep all the women cheerful and optimistic, working hard and doing their best for the company. These problems did hang heavily on her, and she wished there was someone she could share them with. She couldn't share them with her mother, because her mother just wouldn't be able to look at them rationally. It wasn't Elizabeth Trench's style to offer consolation, any more than it would be her style to offer to do a little typing or bookkeeping. Perhaps it was as well, admittedly, that she showed no interest in bookkeeping! Elizabeth Trench's only concern about Trenco just then was to persuade Janis to invite Marcus home for supper; and, so far, Janis had avoided doing that.

It was important to avoid it, because there were several very good reasons why Janis couldn't share her problems with Marcus, either. For a start, she didn't trust him. She still couldn't understand why he had chosen to become involved in Trenco. And, for another thing, she was bitterly opposed to his policies for the company, and she was working directly in opposition to them.

Marcus wanted to keep producing shirts, while Janis was convinced that Trenco desperately needed its overdue change of direction. She had a little less work to do on the company administration, now Marcus was there; and she had been spending the time it gave her on preparing some new designs.

They were all in her studio at White Gates, where Marcus was least likely to see them. Janis had been working on them most evenings. She had also been taking some time off from the factory during the week, though only on the days when Marcus was not there. Her first prototypes were almost ready, and she had an appointment the following week with a store buyer who had been enthusiastic about her descriptions of the garments on the phone. That, too, was on a day when Marcus Anson would not be working at Trenco.

The trouble was, there were only so many hours in the day and, spending most of them on the routine work and the new designs, Janis had had none to spare for the accounting system. She had no idea, she was forced to admit to herself, just how bad Trenco's financial position was. Marcus was steadily taking over the negotiation of the new contracts, working out the costing on his computer, and he was handling all the day-to-day finances. In many ways, Janis was coming to feel that she was as much in the dark as

Mr Jenkins and her mother.

Except that she, unlike them, knew there was reason to worry. And she, unlike them, did not have unlimited trust in Marcus Anson.

Unlike Anthea, too—for Anthea seemed to idolise Marcus, and she jumped instantly to his defence if Janis ever dared to venture a word of criticism. That was one reason why Janis had never tried to look over the figures on the computer on the days when Marcus was out of the office. Anthea, she knew, would have told Marcus about it as soon as he returned.

Perhaps the answer, she thought suddenly, would be to go back to the factory in the evening. She knew enough about the computer to be able to load the accounting programs herself, and then she could check out everything privately, without worrying or upsetting anybody.

The more she thought about it, the more this idea appealed to her. It was a disappointment, almost, to remember that she had promised to go and visit her friend Louise that evening. She thought for a moment of phoning Louise to cancel, but it was a long-standing date, and it wouldn't be fair to do that at short notice.

She was so distant at supper that even her mother noticed it, and commented to her. 'Was Marcus at the office today, Janis?'

'Only this morning,' Janis said shortly. 'Trenco isn't his company, you know, Mother. He has an accountancy partnership to run as well.'

Her mother smiled complacently. 'Maybe that's why you're a little down, dear. Because you miss him when he's not around.'

Oh, yes, I miss him, Janis thought to herself. I miss that feeling of being ganged-up on by him and

Anthea. I miss watching Anthea make his coffee first and type his letters first. I miss his damned computer screen glowing away in the corner. I miss him switching my phone extension to his desk so that he can phone up my customers for me. I could do with missing all that all of the time. If I were missing Marcus Anson, I really would have something to cheer about!

'I had one or two problems in the office today, Mother.'

Her mother was not listening. 'I was thinking, dear, that maybe I ought to invite him here to dinner myself. I mean, I can see it might be a little awkward if you were to do it. He may be a director of the company, but it's not as if he's ever asked you out, is it?'

Janis fought to keep her temper. 'Nor is he likely to, Mother. Really, I do wish you wouldn't try to match-make for me. Marcus Anson isn't my type at all.'

'Oh, it wouldn't be a *date*, dear. Just a friendly evening.'

'I could do without friendly evenings like that.' The reaction this retort received told Janis immediately that she had given away too much. She hurriedly added, 'No, really, Mother. I see him for hours each week as it is. I don't have any interest in seeing still more of him in the evenings, and I'm sure he doesn't want to see any more of me.'

'I still think you're wrong, Janis.'

Janis didn't answer, and they finished their supper in silence. Immediately afterwards, she set off to visit Louise, warning her mother that she might be back late.

Louise lived in a bungalow on the other side of Smithbury, overlooking the cliffs. It was a plain, box-

like little bungalow, but she had made it uniquely her
own with her unusual choice of colours, and with the
mass of her home-fired pots that lined every shelf.
Janis had helped her tie-dye her curtains in a bright
blend of oranges, reds and yellows, and the yellow
walls and deep red carpet brought a shade of Mexican
warmth to the chill English spring evening. It cheered
Janis to enter the house, and yet she could not help
feeling a pang of jealousy. It was so much more like
the kind of home she desired for herself than her
mother's house ever could be—and she seemed so far,
herself, from ever setting up home with a husband she
loved.

Louise had married the previous year, to a young
teacher she had known since her schooldays. Bruce
was off playing squash, and the two women sat at the
kitchen table, talking and playing records while
Louise painted her latest batch of pots with swirly
designs in reds and blues.

Janis tried to push aside her disquiet about her
business, and chattered on instead about the new
designs. Louise listened intently, while she painted
the familiar patterns automatically with practised
hands.

'You don't think,' she said at last, 'that you're
getting a touch too conservative, Janis? I know you
need to produce commercial clothes, stuff for chain
stores, rather than special outfits for boutiques. But
all this talk about beiges and greys? What's wrong
with some nice cheery yellow and blue?'

Janis laughed. Louise would never be caught dead
in beige or grey. Nor was it really her own style. 'I'm
trying to produce a good spread, Louise,' she
explained. 'To offer the buyers a selection, so that
they can choose the colours and designs they prefer.

So some of them are really conventional, and—well, I must admit the ones I like best myself are a little more unusual. But I don't just have to please the buyers. I have to satisfy the bank, too, that I'm not doing something with too much of a risk to it. I think they see bright colours and striking patterns as being risky, somehow.'

'What happens, then? Does the bank manager come round and check over your designs? Give them ticks and crosses? Tell you which ones to work on, and which to scrap?'

Janis giggled. 'Not exactly! But, you know, the bank has a nominee on the board of the company. Two nominees, now. The man who's working with us will obviously see what I'm doing, and make some comments on it. I've done one design for a loose jacket that I was really pleased with. With low-cut shoulders, and a wrapover front. If you have some paper, I'll show you what I mean.'

Louise was not to be fooled. 'When you've told me about "the man". *What* man? Who is he? What's he like?'

The LP they were playing ended just then, and the needle began to scratch round in the last groove. Janis had a moment's respite while she went to change it. She put on some loud Latin-American jazz. 'Turn it down a bit,' Louise said as she returned to the kitchen. 'I can tell when you're hiding something. You don't get away with it that easily.'

Janis flushed. 'I'm not hiding anything,' she retorted. 'It's just that it gets on my nerves, having a man from the bank in the office half the time.'

'Spying on you?'

'Not exactly. Sticking his oar in a bit.'

'I'd have thought you might be grateful. Doing the

accounts never was quite your style, was it?'

'It sure is Mr Anson's.'

' "Mr Anson",' Louise mimicked. 'Very matey. Is he fat, balding and fifty?'

Janis grinned. 'No, he's tall, dark and handsome. Maybe thirty-five. Anthea has a tremendous crush on him.'

'Oh, dear!' teased Louise. 'Only Anthea? Is he married?'

'No,' Janis admitted grudgingly. Anthea had extracted this piece of information on Marcus's first day. 'Nor is he going to marry me,' she added, 'so there's no need to do your imitation of my mother.'

'Ah,' Louise said. 'That must be trying, having your mother trying to pair you off all the time. You ought to get out more, Janis, meet more men, then she wouldn't get so intense about it.'

'Now you really do sound like my mother!'

Louise laughed, and hastily changed the subject.

It was not long after ten when Janis left. Bruce was back from his squash game, looking disgustingly fit and self-satisfied, and he and Louise had waved her goodbye from their doorstep, with their arms around each other. The warm feeling they gave out faded as Janis drove off, and it left behind the miserable knowledge that she had never been more alone. Nor had she ever had more problems that she wished she coud share with someone.

Well, since they could not be shared, they would have to be tackled. She could afford to put in an hour, maybe two, on Mr Anson's computer. She took the ringroad at a sharp forty miles an hour, and by ten-thirty she was swinging her car into the service track that led up to Trenco.

A sudden alarm bell rang in her head as she reached the factory forecourt and, instead of dropping the Mini into her usual parking place, she wrenched the wheel sharply, and drove on to the end of the road. She turned, and looked again to make sure she had not been mistaken.

She wasn't. There was an unfamiliar car parked outside the Trenco factory, a battered soft-top in a dark colour she could not make out in the artificial light. And there was a light shining in the window that gave on to her office.

It seemed too blatant for a burglar. But only she and Anthea had keys to the factory, and Anthea would hardly come back to work late in the evening. The car wasn't Anthea's old Cortina, anyway. The security guards who patrolled the estate might not have bothered to check too carefully, assuming that whoever was there must be working with her permission, or they would have covered their tracks better.

Janis's brain was working overtime. How much petty cash was there in the safe? Perhaps a hundred pounds—and quite a few bankers' orders and giros as well. The computer was well worth stealing, and most of the machines were easily transportable. Admittedly, not much equipment would fit in the battered soft-top, but it might just be a cover for an articulated lorry out at the back of the factory.

The dark and the silence of the estate made her nervous. She drove as slowly and silently as she could manage over to the estate office, and pressed the button that would call the guard back from his patrol.

The guard was a grizzled ex-policeman, with a large Alsatian dog on a short leash at his side. He listened to Janis's story, and promptly picked up the phone.

'Better safe than sorry, love,' he explained. 'And it never does any harm to remind the police we're here.'

The police arrived, in force, ten minutes later. With truncheons, another van full of dogs, and, Janis strongly suspected, a couple of guns. They rapidly surrounded the block of factories. Janis handed over her key. 'Stand well back, love,' the sergeant told her. She hovered in the shadow of the buildings across the road as he unlocked the door, and disappeared into the dimly lit corridor with a couple of his colleagues close at his heels.

There was a tense two minutes' silence. Then the open door blazed with light, and two men appeared, silhouetted sharply against the glare. One was wearing a policeman's hat; one was not.

They marched inexorably, side by side, across the road to where Janis was waiting.

'Perhaps you could explain to this officer, Miss Trench, that I am in our office on perfectly legitimate business, and that there is absolutely no need for all this cops-and-robbers performance.'

Janis didn't need to take in the icy tones to discover that Marcus Anson was very, very angry. With her. She had a desperate urge to turn to the policeman for protection, but that was hardly fair, in the circumstances. She took a deep breath, and managed to stutter out some kind of an explanation.

The sergeant was not prepared to be so easily satisfied. He made them go back into the office, and he pored over Marcus's driving licence, business card and the new company letterhead before he was convinced that Marcus was who he said he was. Then he muttered some uncomfortable remarks about wasting police time, and strode away, calling his men, loudly, to leave off their ambush.

It dawned on Janis that it might have been wiser to follow the police away. Too late. Marcus Anson was already slamming the office door, and she was left to confront him in the blazing light of the little room.

'What a ridiculous, hysterical, histrionic stunt to play!'

Janis suddenly discovered that she was even more angry than she was frightened.

'*Me* play a stunt?' she yelled back. 'How about *your* stunt? Coming up here in the middle of the night, in a strange car, and doing heaven knows what behind my back. Prying through my papers and stealing control of my company from me! *You're* angry? How the hell do you think *I* feel?'

Marcus took a step closer towards her. 'This is not *your* company! Will you never learn, you stupid woman? This is *our* company! I'm a director, too, and I have just as much right as you to be here!'

'That you have not! Hell, you didn't even have a key yesterday!'

'Well, I have one now.'

'Sure you didn't break in? I wouldn't put it past you! Pity I didn't come in with the police, then I might have caught you red-handed, rifling through my desk drawers!'

There was a short, charged silence, before Marcus said icily, 'I have never, ever, given you any reason at all to suspect me of anything like that. And I'm not having you make wild accusations of me. I work my fingers to the bone, trying to pull this damn company back from the brink, and all I get in return is a flood-tide of hatred and distrust. You can have your goddamned key! And don't expect me to work a moment longer for you and your wretched company.' He reached into his pocket, and hurled a key down on to the floor between them. Then he turned and strode from the room, slamming the door behind him.

He was almost at the main door before Janis had wrenched the office door back open, and wailed down the corridor, 'Marcus!'

He paused, then turned and, very slowly, came back up the corridor towards her.

'It is a little late,' he said coldly, 'to offer me an apology.'

'I wasn't.'

'I'm glad to hear it.'

This time, she did not dare to call him back. She stood in the corridor, paralysed, as Marcus strode out to the car on the forecourt. He crunched the gears appallingly as he slammed it into reverse, swept backwards on to the service road, and drove off into the night.

A moment later, Janis recovered enough to move back into the office. The lights were still blazing, illuminating coldly, pitilessly, every detail of the little scene. Her desk, with its chair aligned precisely in the centre, as she had left it that afternoon. Marcus's desk, strewn with papers. The computer, switched to a screen full of the financial forecasts she had come there to check over. Anthea's pots of geraniums, the avocado plants and orange trees. The familiar drawings and posters. And, on the floor, forlorn in the middle of the cord carpet, the spare key.

Janis bent, blindly, to pick it up. It was the key she kept at home. She was sure she had left it in her studio, in the drawer of the old kitchen table she kept up there. She weighed it in her hand, heavy and accusing. Then she collapsed on to the carpet, in a flood of exhausted tears.

The next thing she knew, strong arms were picking

her up off the ground, and holding her in something resembling an upright position. She blundered against a hard male body.

'Oh, God,' said Marcus, 'you're crying! Here. Come here.' He led her, gently, to his desk, sat down on his chair, and pulled her on to his knee. She moved with him, unresisting, buried her head in the dark material of his suit, and cried some more.

There was something wonderful comforting about the firm feel of Marcus's arms around her, and the deep sound of his voice, whispering reassurance to her. His face was buried somewhere in her hair, and as the sobs died down she breathed in his heady male smell of sweat, soap and spicy aftershave.

His hands moved gently across her back, stroking and caressing her; his mouth moved slowly down to her temple, and the touch of it made her raise her face to his. He kissed her eyelids, her lashes, her cheek, tracing the tracks of her tears, drying them. Then he kissed her on the mouth, firmly and confidently, and her lips parted in a sudden urge to take from him all the comfort and reassurance he could give her.

His arms tightened around her, and his questing tongue sent flames snaking through her body, lighting unfamiliar fires deep inside her. His mouth moved down to her neck, biting gently, branding, possessing, and as she moved to welcome his touch and bring her own arms round his shoulders she felt his hand reach to cup her breast.

'Janis . . . Janis.' His mouth claimed hers again, and a little moan escaped her as he unbuttoned her blouse, and his fingers slipped under the edge of her bra. They teased and caressed the mound of her breast, circling the tip, turning the nipple into a hard, aching knot of desire. She leaned backwards, feeling his arm take her weight, sensing him shift on the chair, moving to settle beneath her. His leg came between hers, and her body arched upwards, pressing against his thigh, melting against his hardness as a hot flood of longing invaded her.

'Is everything all right here?'

The sudden voice at the door made them both start guiltily to their feet. The guard's head poked cautiously round the door. 'You left the main door open,' he added accusingly. 'Just wanted to make sure that there was no problems.'

'No, not at all,' Marcus said, in a voice that seemed to Janis to be uncannily steady. 'The lady's a little upset. It was a big shock to her.'

'She's left her car over by the main gate. You going to drive her over and pick it up?'

'In a minute,' Marcus agreed. 'As soon as we've locked up here.'

'I'll be expecting you,' the guard said. He withdrew, and they stood, inches apart, listening to his footsteps fading into the distance.

"Are you OK now?' said Marcus.

Janis did not dare to meet his gaze. She felt far from OK. Her legs were unsteady, her body trembling. But she managed a nod, and then turned from him to button up her blouse and tuck it back into her skirt. Behind her, she could hear the whirr of the computer-disc drives as he prepared to shut down the system.

'Would you like the key back?' he asked in a low voice.

'Keep it,' she whispered.

He took her arm and led her out of the office, through the deserted reception area. When they reached the main door, he stopped to turn off all the lights behind them, and to lock up the factory. He slipped the key into his pocket, and helped Janis into the battered car.

He parked, neatly, next to her own car at the main gate. The guard looked out from his open doorway, and gave them a wave of acknowledgement.

'I'll see you in the morning.'

Janis nodded silently.

'Are you OK to drive? Would you like me to take you home?'

'No. No, I'll drive.'

'Be careful.' He reached over to hold her face in his hands, and leaned forward, kissing her again, very gently, full on the lips. Then he released her, and reached over to unfasten the door, and let her out of the car.

He waited there while she climbed into her car and started it, nervously. As she pulled on to the main road, she saw him drive up behind her, flash his lights in brief acknowledgement, and then turn away in the opposite direction, towards the town.

CHAPTER FOUR

'IT WAS a pity you were out last evening, Janis,' Elizabeth Trench said brightly over breakfast. 'Because Marcus called round.'

Janis looked up from her toast, heavy-eyed. 'Did he?' she replied dutifully.

'Not that he stayed for long. Though I expect he would have had a cup of coffee at least, if you'd been here.'

At least, Janis echoed to herself. 'What did he want?' she made herself ask.

'To borrow the key to the factory, dear. I knew you wouldn't mind. In fact, to be honest, Janis, I was a little surprised that you hadn't already given him one of his own.'

'Were you?' Janis thought again. 'Did he go up to the studio?' she asked.

'Only for a minute. I told him I didn't know where you kept the key, but it seemed he found it without any trouble.' Elizabeth smiled happily across the table, and then took in something of her daughter's expression. 'Oh, Janis, there's no need to pout at me like that! Marcus must know by now how much you hate people messing with your work. I'm sure he wouldn't have touched any of your drawings.'

Janis gazed back, horror-struck. The rest of the toast seemed to stick to the roof of her mouth. She swallowed it hastily, gulping great mouthfuls of tea to wash it down and, quickly excusing herself, rushed up to the attic studio.

Her portfolio lay open on the side table, with a couple of sketches that she had colourwashed the day before uppermost. A deep yellow shirtdress with a blue belt, and another, low-waisted, tentatively coloured a pale mint green. Spread out across the floor were the pieces of her prototype pattern, pinned to an accusing expanse of scarlet flannel material. On her easel, she had left the sketch of the wrapover jacket she had mentioned to Louise. The sketch was exaggerated, in classic fashion-drawing style, and the model had wide shoulders and an imperious face. She would not have looked out of place in one of the posh Sunday papers, or in the fashion report pages of *Vogue;* in Eastbourne Road she would definitely have merited a few astonished looks! Tucked under one of the paperclips was a scrap torn from her phone pad, with a message in bold black writing. 'Have borrowed the factory key. MA.'

Janis freed the note, and stood for a moment, gazing down at it. The confident, slashed lines of Marcus's handwriting brought back with painful clarity the memory of his touch the night before. His hands, roving, arousing, possessing. His mouth.

In a quarter of an hour, she would have to go back to the factory and face him, in the very place where he had kissed and caressed her. She felt raw and exposed, both mentally and physically. In one evening, he had uncovered everything about her that she had intended to keep from him. Her ideas, her hopes. Her desires. Heavens, how appallingly clear she had made it that she desired him! She had uncovered knowledge about herself, too, that she had never been forced to face before. Patrick had never unleashed in her that sweet, unstoppable flood of passion.

It was a flood, surely, that had swept him along, too. Or had it? All night long, Janis had replayed the scene in the office, first from one angle, then from the other. Marcus the lover, holding her in his arms, sharing her hopes and her fears, giving her help and encouragement. Giving her joy. And Marcus the enemy, the dangerous man who was trying to wrest control of her company from her, suddenly seizing his greatest advantage yet, and waiting now, to capitalise on it. She had no idea which man she was about to encounter.

Janis closed her hand around Marcus's note, and dropped it, carefully, into her overflowing wastebin. She went back to the bathroom, and splashed her face yet again with cold water. She popped into the kitchen only for as long as it took to grab her sandwiches and call out 'See you this evening' to her mother. When she reached her car, she was forced to clench her hands on the wheel and mentally shake herself before she could bring herself to drive off.

She was ten minutes late. Outside Trenco, the car Marcus had driven the night before—dark green, in daylight—was already parked next to Anthea's Cortina. Janis tested her smile in the rear-view mirror, decided that it would not stand up to even a cursory inspection, and let her face droop. If Anthea asked, she told herself, she would plead a thumping headache.

Marcus glanced up from his computer screen as she walked in, and their eyes met momentarily. The little flash of electricity that burned through Janis was becoming painfully familiar. There was no smile around his mouth, either, and he greeted her tersely, brushing his hair back from his forehead in the mannerism he used when he was edgy.

'Morning,' Anthea said cheerily. 'Coffee, Janis?'

'Strong. Black. With an aspirin.'

'Ah! One of those mornings. How was he?' Janis stared at her blankly, and she added, 'Your date? You weren't out late on your own, surely?'

'No. With my friend Louise and her husband.'

Anthea shrugged. 'Takes all sorts. Well, you missed all the excitement here.'

'Excitement?'

Anthea brought over the coffee, and perched on the edge of Janis's desk. 'Harry, the maintenance man, says there was a robbery on the estate last night. He's not sure where, yet. But they had the police here in force, with dogs and all, and caught them red-handed.'

'Did they?' Marcus's deep voice saved Janis from thinking of a response.

'So Harry said. He's going to tell me more at lunch time.'

'Are there many robberies around here?' Marcus asked.

'Always are on estates like this, aren't there? Especially at Watson's. You know, where they make the car radios. They get two or three break-ins a year. We've only had the one, haven't we, Janis? That time when you came in early and found the office wrecked.'

'You found . . .'

There was an unfamiliar edge to Marcus's voice, and Janis was forced to reply. 'It was just over a year ago,' she said quickly. 'Shortly after I started working for my father. It wasn't as bad as it might have been. An amateur job, the police said. They didn't get into the safe, but they threw some papers around, and stole a typewriter. Oh, and the kettle! It was really the shock that was the worst, coming in early in the morning and finding the place turned upside-down, when it had looked so normal from the outside.'

'You ought to have an alarm system,' Marcus said.

'We did think of it, but it's hardly a deterrent in a place like this. By the time the police respond, the thieves are usually away. Though they did say that, if I ever had any suspicion of trouble again, I was to call them as fast as I could.'

'Very wise,' Marcus agreed.

'I suppose the computer would make us quite a target now . . .'

'Not really. Computers are so cheap these days, and there's not much of a second-hand market in them, so they're hard for thieves to dispose of. And, if it was stolen, we could recover quickly, since all the files are duplicated on disks. We really should keep a spare set of disks somewhere else, though, just in case vandals wreck both the sets here. In my office, perhaps.'

Janis felt a little pang of annoyance. Computers and disks were such prosaic things to be talking about. Not that they could have had a great passionate encounter, with Anthea watching, but all the same it hurt. Not by a glance or a gesture, since that first look, had Marcus the lover shown himself; and Marcus the enemy was still waiting there to be uncovered under every sentence. What must seem to Anthea to be an innocuous suggestion hinted to Janis of hidden traps and snares. Why should they keep the duplicate computer records in his office? It was foreign territory, closed to her. He had exposed so much of her, he had invaded her own office and had even explored her studio behind her back, and yet she had never passed beyond the little brass plaque of Anson and Williams. 'My studio, perhaps,' she retorted.

'That would do just as well.' He hesitated. 'It really

would be wise, too, if somebody else knew about the system. I was wondering if you could spare some time this morning to go over it with me.'

A morning working with Marcus. Sitting shoulder to shoulder, listening to his deep, velvety voice, watching his confident hands, meeting his eyes as he explained his system to her. Blundering deeper and deeper into his trap. Oh, no! Especially not in front of Anthea.

'Maybe tomorrow,' Janis said brusquely. 'I have some orders to check over this morning.'

'I won't be in tomorrow. But it can wait.' He turned back to his computer, pressed some keys, and concentrated fiercely on the screen. Janis emptied her coffee-cup rapidly, and disappeared into the storeroom with a sheaf of orders in her hand.

Just before twelve-thirty, the storeroom door opened. Janis whirled round, alarmed, and found Marcus standing there.

'Leave that for now,' he said. 'I'm taking you out to lunch.'

'But I have to . . .'

'It can wait. I'll help you this afternoon, if it's urgent.'

He took a few steps into the storeroom, and reached out a hand to her cheek. His fingers brushed across it. A traitorous surge of joy ran through her. Lunch with Marcus. The two of them together. Then he said abruptly, 'Go and tidy up. I'll wait for you by the car.'

In the cloakroom, Janis discovered that there was a big sooty smear on her cheek, where Marcus had touched her. She rubbed it away, smiling ruefully at her wilder imaginings of his motives, put on some lipstick and then wiped it off again, and dashed through the office with a murmur to Anthea.

He drove her to an Italian restaurant in the centre of town. Round the corner from his office, she realised, as the waiter greeted him by name and showed them to a window table. He ordered veal, repeating her order of a salad without comment, poured her a glass of fizzy mineral water, and said abruptly, 'Anthea told me you've been working at home on the days when I'm not at the factory.'

His manner now was sharp, businesslike and faintly accusing. Janis, who had half expected accusations, was still caught off balance by his line of attack. She retorted, 'So what?'

'So you've been hiding that from me.'

'I'm not hiding anything! I've always had a studio at home. I had it even before I began to work for Trenco. I don't have the space to design at the factory, or the peace. I always do my designing there.'

'On the days when I'm not around to notice.'

That was so patently true that Janis could hardly deny it. 'I do it mainly in the evenings,' she replied. 'I've taken a day a week from the factory, at the very most. And that's only because you've taken over so much of the work I used to do.'

Marcus ignored this gibe. 'We agreed,' he said, 'that we were going to concentrate on the shirts. At least until the company is on a proper footing again. You are breaking our agreement.'

'*Our* agreement!' Janis's voice began to rise, and Marcus's hand came up to remind her that they were in a crowded restaurant. She lowered it again, with an effort, and went on, 'That has never been our agreement. It's your policy, imposed on me.'

'It's the policy,' he said, 'of the board, as agreed by me, Jenkins and your mother. A three-to-one majority decision. I decide which contracts we take on, and at what prices. I decide how we allocate our resources.'

'I've hardly used any of Trenco's resources on my designing. I've done all the work at home. I bought the material for making up the samples. And I haven't even made up samples of most of the designs.'

'But you,' Marcus persisted, 'are Trenco's most valuable resource. I am not having you waste your time on these ridiculous schoolgirl sketches, when you ought to be working on our contract work. I forbid it. Is that understood?'

'They are not schoolgirl sketches!' The waiter arrived just then, and Janis waited, edgily, as he served them before she continued in a hiss, 'They are my new season's designs. I already have store buyers interested in looking at them.'

Marcus snorted. *'Looking!'*

'And quite possibly giving us orders for them.'

'Janis.' Marcus was in control now, deliberately even-voiced and rational as Janis was growing more and more furious. 'I may not know much about fashion, but you can't fool me that those ridiculous drawings I saw in your studio have anything to do with the kind of clothes that are sold in Smithbury High Street and Eastbourne Road.'

'Of course they are! That's just the style of fashion drawings. The clothes always look exaggerated. Made up, they'll be just the kind of clothes that I wear, or Anthea, or anybody else.'

Marcus did not even glance at Janis's outfit. In fact, she had put on a plain blue woollen dress that morning, deliberately non-provocative. It was not, unfortunately, one of her own designs.

'When we turn the corner,' he persisted, 'then maybe we'll have a chance to diversify slightly. With well made, classic clothes in sensible colours. But I am not, not, repeat *not*, going to allow you to waste your time on these ludicrous cartoons.'

'I'll spend my time exactly how I choose.'

'Your time, perhaps. Trenco's time, you spend how I choose.'

'I'll resign!'

'I got that line in first. Yesterday.' He leaned towards her. 'And you can't resign, for the same reason that I can't. Because, without both of us, Trenco wouldn't survive a month; and because you can't afford to let it collapse.'

It was all too painfully true. So painfully true that it almost—but not quite—masked Marcus's other meaning. That his reasons for staying with Trenco were practical ones. His only reasons. And that Janis had been hopelessly, idiotically deluded in ever imagining for a second that it might have been otherwise.

She put her hands up to her face for a moment, unable to look across the table at him.

'All right,' Marcus said. 'Let's drop it. That's all I wanted to say. You haven't started your lunch.'

He began on his veal as he spoke, and Janis, taking a deep breath, lowered her hands and took a sip of the fizzy water. It was an Italian brand, slightly bitter, which tasted utterly revolting to her. She glanced around them, caught one or two curious glances, and picked up her knife and fork. They must think, she thought bitterly, that we're having a lover's tiff. And here we are, instead, the businesswoman in a mess and the accountant who is trying to steal her business, in the guise of saving it!

Somehow, they got through the rest of the meal, talking platitudes about the weather, the summer show at Smithbury Theatre, the difficulties of parking in town. Marcus played squash in the evenings, Janis learned. He had a flat in a block not far from his office. He was planning to sell the green soft-top as soon as it was in a reasonable state, but he intended to hold on to the vintage Jaguar he had been driving on the day they met. She clung jealously to these scraps of information. He knew so much about her, and she still barely seemed to know him at all.

'I have to call in at my office,' he told her, when the waiter offered them coffee. 'I'll make you a cup there.' He handed over a credit card, and she smarted a little at his airy assumption that he would pay the bill. Though it had been his idea, she reminded herself, that they eat out. She would have to throw away her sandwiches on the way home.

Anson and Williams turned out to be a larger outfit than Janis had envisaged. She had imagined a little two-man office around the size of hers and Anthea's, but instead there was a plushy reception area and a large open-plan workspace dissected by bright orange screens. Behind them, she glimpsed half a dozen people at work, though it was still not quite two o'clock, and several desks were empty. Marcus swept her towards a mahogany door, firmly closed, and stopped to ask a pretty red-haired secretary sitting just outside—wearing a wedding ring, Janis couldn't help noticing—to bring them coffee. So much for making her a cup himself, Janis thought, amused in spite of herself.

Behind the mahogany door, his office was large and airy. It was thoroughly businesslike: no empty expanses of executive desk, but an array of computers and printers, stacks of neat files, a wall lined with bookshelves, all crammed to overflowing. Nearer the window there were three or four low leather chairs,

and a heavy glass coffee-table, covered with news-
papers and financial magazines. It was luxurious, but
compared to her own office it was impersonal: there
were no flowers, no family photos, no prints on the
walls. She crossed to the window. They were higher
up than she had realised, and she could look down,
over the roofs of lower Smithbury, towards the beach,
the pier and the sea.

'That's what I miss most at Trenco,' Marcus said,
close behind her. 'Seeing the sea. We picked these
offices because I was absolutely determined to have
a sea view. I'd like you to have a view like this
one.'

'So would I,' Janis agreed. Turning, she was so near
to him that a casual movement could easily have
brought them into contact. She stood there for a
moment, almost hypnotised by his closeness; and then
the door opened, and the secretary brought in a tray of
coffee.

The secretary had half a dozen letters for Marcus to
look over and sign, a few urgent phone calls to draw to
his attention and, drifting towards his desk, Marcus
had soon switched on his computer and was absorbed
in his work. Janis poured the coffee, brought him over
a cup, drank her own, flicked through the *Financial
Times* and the *Guardian*. A colleague came in with a
problem, was dealt with, and disappeared again. She
was conscious of the efficiency of his words and move-
ments, of the speed with which he seemed to unearth
the core of the problems that came up, and solve
them. She realised, belatedly, that she was staring at
him. Dragging her eyes away, she stood up and went
over to look at his bookshelves.

The titles meant nothing to her, but she was in a
kind of trance, deliberately closing her mind to

Marcus and his actions. It came as a shock to her when his hands descended on her shoulders, and he brought her gently round to face him. They were alone, she realised. The door was shut, and the computer had been switched off. It was very quiet in the room.

'You're still mad at me?'

In her high-heeled pumps, she was only a couple of inches shorter than he was, and she had to look down to avoid his eyes. He seemed to take her gesture for a nod of agreement.

'Don't be,' he whispered, and drew her closer. Her hands came out, as if to push him away, but he ignored them, and Janis found herself moving them around to his back, in her sudden urgency to complete their embrace.

He held her tightly, crushing her to him, and his mouth roved across her temples, drifted lightly across her lashes, teased its way down the curve of her nose, and finally found her own mouth with arrogant certainty. His hands loosed their grip a fraction, and she eased her body up and against his, finding the perfect match to every curve and hollow.

His mouth freed hers and then claimed it again, with a growing urgency that brought an instant response from her. The blood was hammering in her ears, her heartbeat echoed the thud of his. She shifted against him, and his hands, moving deliberately down from her waist, pulled her hips hard up to meet his, so that she was unavoidably conscious of his growing arousal. She swayed against him, blindly echoing his desire, inviting him on, and as he dropped his head to nuzzle the hollow at the base of her neck she heard his low, animal groan.

Suddenly, he was pushing her away, gently but firmly; shaken, and panting slightly, Janis collapsed against the wall of bookshelves.

'Marcus.' In her voice, desire blended with uncertainty, longing with a barely acknowledged fear.

'We'd better go,' he said curtly. He crossed to the door and waited by it, until Janis had recovered herself enough to join him and make her way out through the main office.

He barely spoke on their way back to the factory; and when they reached it he disappeared rapidly towards the office, leaving Janis to return alone to her work in the storeroom. When she emerged, Anthea told her—with a curious glance that made her wonder just how much Harry had discovered about the goings-on the night before—that Marcus had already left.

'Janis.' Louise's voice on the phone was bright and determined, firmly closed to argument. 'Your mother's already told me you're free for Friday night, so there's no escape. Bruce's friend, Roger—you know Roger, don't you?—is holding a barbecue down on the beach, and you're to come with us. There'll be a couple of dozen people, and they aren't all paired off, so you won't feel left out. Though, if you did have someone to bring . . .'

'I might,' Janis said cautiously.

'Well, if you do, fine, and if you don't, you never know who you might meet. Lots of hunky men from the squash club, Bruce says.'

'Mmm,' Janis said, absently. Her mind was full of images of Marcus. Marcus at the office, dark-suited and arrogant, automatically and inevitably in control of everyone and everything. Marcus playing squash, in little white shorts, showing a long expanse of muscular thigh. Marcus swimming at the beach.

Marcus in bed. She pulled herself together, and asked Louise what time the barbecue was.

'Come round here about eight,' Louise told her. 'A group of us are meeting here and going down together. And if you could get your mother to make one of her cheesecakes . . .'

Janis laughed. 'Now, what I really need,' she said, 'is a nice man for my mother. Not hunky, exactly. Say, fifty to sixty-five, executive type, fond of home life, maybe a bridge player . . .'

'I'll work on it,' Louise said briskly, 'if it'll get you out more. You need a man, Janis. That would get some inspiration into your designs.'

'It's hardly inspiration I need now, Louise, just time. I'm seeing the buyer from Vane's next Tuesday, and I've only got one of my samples made up.'

'Do it Saturday,' Louise said. 'There's plenty of time. And be sure to come with us on Friday. If you don't, we'll call round and haul you away from that studio of yours!'

Janis let out a long mock groan, and promised yet again to come. It did sound like fun, she had to admit, when she had put the telephone down. At least, it *would* be fun, if Marcus was there. It was hard to work up much enthusiasm, just then, for anything that didn't involve Marcus.

At the same time, she knew her problems were far from over. She was painfully aware that Marcus's kisses by no means implied Marcus's love. They were more a gesture of possession, of victory. One more way of ensuring that she would do as he said—as he ordered, rather. She had the feeling that he had seen the interlude in his office as a way of breaking down her resistance, rather than the start of a romance. He had left Trenco, after all, without any hint that he wanted to see her outside office hours. There had been no message on her desk, no phone call that evening, no call the following day. There had been no words of love, nothing that might compromise his damnable professional ethics.

Now it was Wednesday evening, and Marcus would be in the office on Thursday. On Friday there would be the beach barbecue, and on the following Tuesday Janis would be seeing the buyer from Vane's, at the company's London headquarters, She had already prepared the ground for that, ensured that it would be on one of Marcus's days at Anson and Williams, and that Anthea believed she was taking the day off to have her hair done. Which she would, as part of her elaborate cover.

Her cover had improved since Marcus had made his discoveries. She hadn't given in, decided to follow his policies—oh, no! She had accepted, though, that there could be no more days working at home. The only days she would spend away from the factory would be those when she had appointments—all carefully arranged on away ground—with fashion buyers. She would prepare her samples in the evenings, at home. If she did receive any small, initial orders, she would do those, too, in the evenings when Marcus was not around to see. She could pay Stella to help her, and one or two of the other women who she could trust not to tell Marcus. Marcus would only find out what she had been doing when she was finally in a position to present him with a large, fat, undeniable contract.

There were quite a few weak points in this plan, Janis freely admitted. There was her painful attraction to Marcus, for instance. She knew it was entirely probable that Marcus would guess what she was planning, and ask her out, simply to make sure that she wouldn't have time to put her plans into action. After the way she'd acted when he kissed her, he would certainly smell a rat if she refused him—if she managed to summon the will-power to refuse him at all.

Certainly, she couldn't ask him out herself, even to something as innocent as a beach barbecue. It had been a weak-willed indulgence even to think of it for a moment. It might distract him a little, but it would take up too much of her precious time, and it would mean Marcus would have an excuse to come to her house, and then he might want to look at her studio. By then, the evidence of her work would be too much to hide.

The other problem was her mother. Marcus was wrong, of course, in suggesting that Elizabeth Trench sided with him and against her daughter. She was not really doing anything of the kind. It was just that she still had not realised that there was any kind of a battle going on for control of Trenco. She imagined, poor naïve Mother, that Janis and Marcus were on the same side, and that she could give them both the same indulgent smiles, put her complete trust in both of them.

Janis could not possibly afford, at this delicate stage, to disabuse her mother. At the first hint of real trouble, her mother was only too likely to go rushing to Mr Jenkins in search of an alternative source of reassurance. Janis had peeped at Marcus's figures the previous evening, and knew very well now that they were quite as bad as she feared, and not likely to reassure Mr Jenkins in the slightest. So Elizabeth must be appeased, distracted, even induced to invite Marcus home for dinner on a night after the Vane's buyer had been dealt with, when Janis would have time to hide away her sketches and her prototypes and would be able to show Marcus up to the studio with perfect safety. Except, if he then took her in his arms, and—oh dear, she thought, not for the first time, it was going to be very, very difficult to get through the next few weeks without betraying herself to him.

CHAPTER FIVE

BALANCING her mother's best cherry cheescake in her hand, and squeezing a bottle of wine under her arm, Janis reached out to ring the bell of Louise and Bruce's bungalow. She wasn't late, but neither was she the first to arrive, she could tell: there was an unfamiliar car in the drive, and there were sounds of loud voices and occasional laughs coming from the front room.

Louise appeared a moment later, resplendent in a long purple caftan.

'Wow, you look amazing!' Janis said.

'Don't I?' Louise laughed. 'I bought it in a jumble sale last weekend. I was determined to wear it tonight, but Bruce keeps insisting it's totally unsuitable, and I need something—well, something like you're wearing.'

Janis glanced down. Her tight-fitting jeans and bright green sweater were not exactly in the same style league, though they were more fitted, she had to agree, to a beach barbecue on a chilly April evening. 'It should be all right, if you don't plan to do any of the cooking,' she said.

'That's what I keep telling Bruce. Anyway, you'll back me up, won't you? Since I'm determined.'

'Since you're determined,' Janis agreed, following Louise into the front room. She glanced around. Bruce was there, of course, lanky and tow-haired, always looking as if he'd just finished a hard day at the farm instead of one at the local comprehensive. Mary and Andy, a couple of old friends. And another man, stocky and dark, whom she didn't know, and who had to be with the stunning blonde standing by the window.

'Hi, Janis. Hand over the supplies, I'll pop them in our car boot now.' Bruce peeped in the bag, and grinned appreciatively when he saw its contents. 'You know everyone, don't you?'

'I don't think we've met,' said the stocky, dark man. 'I'm Peter Williams.' He held out a firm hand, and gestured over to the blonde. 'And my wife, Cheryl.'

Janis introduced herself, since Bruce had already disappeared with the cheesecake, and asked if Peter was a fellow teacher of Bruce's. Bruce met most of his friends through the school, she knew.

Peter shook his head. 'Half right. Cheryl teaches English at Smithbury High, but really, we came along tonight because of the squash club connection.'

'Oh, of course. Louise said this was a squash club do.'

'Not an official one, but Roger's one of those men who spends half his time on the courts or hanging around the club bar. All the squash club regulars come along to his parties.'

'And you're a regular?' Janis's eyes could not help drifting down to Peter's undeniably plump waistline.

Peter laughed. 'Heavens, no! I gave up years ago. My partner's a member, and he keeps us in touch with the club crowd.'

'Your partner?'

'Peter's an accountant,' Cheryl explained. 'Partner in a little two-man business.'

'Not that little, darling,' Peter protested.

'All right,' smiled Cheryl, continuing what was

clearly a familiar joke between them, 'a dynamic, fast-expanding two-man business.'

'I never thought of accountants as all that dynamic,' said Louise, who was listening.

'That only proves that you don't know Marcus,' said Cheryl.

'Which reminds me, where *is* Marcus? He's not usually late,' Peter said.

Marcus! Marcus Anson—Anson and Williams—Peter Williams. Janis's insides did a very strange somersault, and seemed to return to somewhere quite other than their usual place.

'It's probably Emily,' Cheryl was saying. 'He would have gone to pick her up first, and you know what ages she can take to get ready.'

'Even for a beach barbecue?'

'Well, even for a barbecue, darling, she has to get her hair done, and fix her false eyelashes, and paint her fingernails, and . . .'

'That's Emily!' laughed Peter.

Janis murmured something, and drifted a pace or two away. Then that didn't seem quite enough, so she kept on drifting, and on, until she came to a halt in the kitchen.

'I have a terrible feeling,' said Louise, very quietly, at her side, 'that this is going to be ghastly. Judging from the timing, the reason has to be Marcus.'

Janis gave a miserable nod.

'I'm sure you've never mentioned him.' Janis didn't reply, and Louise said, 'Come on. Tell me quick, and then it'll be over with, and it won't seem quite so awful when he turns up with Emily. At least you'll have my shoulder to cry on, without having to explain all over again.'

Janis gave a wavery smile. 'The trouble is,' she said,

'that I seem to have done quite a bit of crying on Marcus's shoulder recently.'

'About the man from the bank?' asked Louise, hopping on to the edge of the kitchen table.

'Not exactly. Well, the thing is, Marcus *is* the man from the bank. I mean, he's the man from the accountant's, but the bank sent him, and—oh dear, this is awfully complicated.'

'It sure sounds it,' Louise agreed.

'But you mustn't, mustn't, mustn't tell him anything about my designing, Louise. You know nothing about it. You know nothing about me meeting buyers, because as far as he's concerned that's all off. And Bruce doesn't know anything, either. Please?'

'Of course, Janis. Scout's honour. I'll warn Bruce, first chance I get. But I'm still not sure I have this straight. Is this a business feud, or is it an affair of the heart, as they say?'

Janis turned a wide-open, rather damp gaze on her. 'Both,' she said, bleakly. 'Oh, Louise, I think I'd better just turn and run!'

'Nonsense,' Louise said. 'The beach is a big place. You can lose him there if you need to, and go and cry under the cliff. And now, I think a good stiff glass of cooking brandy is called for. In fact, I'll have one myself as well, to keep you company. Bruce is driving,' she added, reaching under the sink for the bottle. 'Not that he knows it yet, but I'd better warn him pretty soon. Cheers!'

'Cheers.' Janis took a big gulp of the brandy, and choked as it went down. She was just recovering when Bruce threw open the kitchen door.

'Marcus and Emily are here,' he said cheerfully, 'so we're just leaving. I say, there's nothing wrong here, is there, girls?'

'We're fine,' Louise said, sweeping off the table and taking Janis's arm. 'Aren't we, Janis?'

'Fine.' Janis gave him a blank, expansive grin. 'Oh, and Bruce—you're driving.'

Squashed in the back of Bruce and Louise's car, with Mary and Andy next to her, Janis didn't have the time or space to think very much about Marcus. There had been just a glimpse of the blue Jaguar outside Louise's bungalow, but he had already got into Peter's car before she'd emerged from the kitchen, and she hadn't had to face him yet. Or Emily, of the false eyelashes and nail varnish.

And she did have the advantage over him this time, she thought wryly to herself, as the car scrunched over the stones of the cliff car park. She had already suffered the worst of the shock, and recovered from it in private. Now she could pick her moment to surprise him in return. At the very least, he would be a little embarrassed, surely. She had never seen him embarrassed or off balance. There might be a kind of painful satisfaction in it.

She stayed close to the others as they loaded up with the supplies from the car boot, and set off down the narrow path that zigzagged from the cliff top to the beach. They were a couple of miles outside the town, on a quiet stretch that had always been popular for barbecues, midnight swimming parties and the like. It had nothing to recommend it except for its quietness: there were no amenities of any kind, and the beach itself was shingly and strewn with seaweed.

It was just about dusk, and the light of the big barbecue fire shone out strongly against the yellowish grey tone of the stones and the greenish grey of the sea. A dozen people were already drifting round it, preparing sausages and burgers, pouring beer from barrels into plastic glasses, waving toasting forks and clowning about. Country music was blaring from a couple of portable speakers. There was the weird, slightly acrid tang of seaweed and driftwood burning, mixed in with the charcoal smell. It was a still evening, and the sea was almost flat, the tide well out.

She saw Marcus straight away. He was standing with Peter and Cheryl and Emily, with his back to her. He looked tall and strong and confident, and Janis's heart leaped and hammered at the sight of him. She edged around to the other side of Bruce, so that she could move closer to him unnoticed. Emily shifted a little, and she made out the streaks in the other girl's expensively cut blonde hair, and a pert, laughing face. Emily was wearing a long skirt, flaring over high boots, and a leather jacket, zipped up to show just the collar of a white blouse. She was heavily made-up, but stylishly so; she looked like an actress playing a cowgirl in a high-class western. Marcus might have been her cowboy, lean and casual in jeans and a denim jacket.

Peter turned, saw Bruce, and called them over.

'Let's drop all this stuff first,' Louise said, elbowing Janis onwards.

'OK.' They went to find Roger, standing by the beer barrels. They handed over their food, uncorked a couple of bottles of wine, and poured themselves drinks. Janis, plastic cup of wine in hand, moved away from the others, and found some different acquaintances to talk to.

When she had worked her way to the other side of the fire, she reckoned it might be safe to glance towards him.

He was looking straight at her. As soon as her eyes

reached him, they connected with his, and a current of fire ran through her. He turned and said something to Emily, who did not glance in Janis's direction, and then he was moving around the end of the barbecue, and towards her.

She could hardly move off without giving away too much, but she did not move towards him, either. He came straight up to her, and stopped barely a foot away. She was wearing flat-soled sneakers, and he seemed taller than she remembered, towering over her.

'Your friend Louise,' he said with a smile, 'and my squash club. We really should have worked this one out, shouldn't we?'

'I can't say I thought about it,' Janis said stiffly.

'Nor did I, or I wouldn't have brought Emily. Come and meet her.'

There was no answer to this, particularly with Marcus reaching out to take her hand. Her arm would have done, Janis thought angrily, as he drew her through the crowd surrounding the fire. There was something painfully intimate about the touch of his bare skin on hers. He kept on holding her hand as he introduced her to Emily, apparently oblivious to her attempts to pull it free.

If Emily noticed this, she didn't seem to mind. Perhaps she was used to Marcus's flirtations with other women, Janis thought to herself. They probably fell over themselves in droves every time he glanced at them. Janis, to Emily, would be just one more idiot, caught in the fringes of Marcus's magic web.

Louise certainly noticed. She raised her eyebrows when nobody else was looking in her direction, and gave Janis a quirky look. Janis tried to inject a plea for help into her return look, and her spirits sank when

Louise grinned at her and disappeared in the direction of the barbecue.

Bruce and Emily and Peter were all talking at once, unable to decide which was the more amazing, that Marcus and Janis should be working together, or that they should never have met otherwise. They'd only just missed each other so often in the past. Of course, quite a few of the men who were good friends at the squash club had barely met each other's wives and girlfriends. They really must have a dinner together, the whole group of them, Peter was saying. Him and Cheryl, Marcus and Emily, Bruce and Louise, Andy and Mary, Janis and . . .

'And Sean,' Bruce said triumphantly. He'd been trying to pair off Janis with his best friend Sean for years, and never had been able to understand that, though Janis was fond of Sean, he had never attracted her physically.

'You and Sean are . . .?' Marcus turned to Janis, and his fingers dug into her palm. She couldn't avoid his look, or stop herself shaking her head.

'How about Roger?' Emily said. There was something a little forced in her voice, over-bright, and Janis, turning her head guiltily away from Marcus, was suddenly aware that, however well the other girl was coping, the situation must be acutely embarrassing for her.

'Now, Roger would——'

'Speak of the devil,' Bruce said cheerfully, interrupting Marcus before Janis could discover his opinion of Roger. 'Here's the man with Louise.'

Louise and Roger were indeed moving towards them, deep in conversation. They broke it off as they approached, the others moved around to make a place for them in the group, and they slid easily into the main conversation. In a moment, it was all arranged. Peter and Cheryl would host the party, in exactly a month from then.

Janis finally rescued her hand and turned to Roger, hoping to draw him away from the others a little. She would gratefully accept the escape route Louise had provided for her for one night, but she also wanted to worm out of the long-term arrangement. Roger had no interest in dating her, she knew: they had been out together for a short while a few years before, and had rapidly found that they had nothing in common. But Roger had already cornered Emily, and was moving off with her in the direction of the cliffs.

'I think the food is ready,' Louise said. 'Come on, Janis, let's dig into the chicken legs before the men beat us to it.'

Louise and Bruce, Marcus and Janis all sat close together on the shingle, a little distance away from the fading barbecue fire. Bruce had his arm round Louise, and she was leaning against him drowsily, singing along slightly out of key to Roger's favourite old Bob Marley tape. Marcus had his arm round Janis. How this had come about, she was not quite sure, but she hadn't been able to do anything about it, not with Louise and Bruce in earshot the whole time. There was such a guilty pleasure in fitting her head into the hollow of his shoulder, feeling the warmth of him next to her, and reaching out a hand to trace a line down the rough denim covering his inner thigh. His arm tightened when she did this, and he bent to whisper something, but his words were lost on the little breeze that was blowing up before she could catch them.

Emily was still with Roger. Janis could see them,

silhouetted against the light from the glowing embers, talking animatedly, waving their glasses in the air, moving close together and then a little apart, touching sometimes, as if by accident. They looked, she had to admit, extraordinarily as if they were perfectly happy to be together. Emily had barely glanced in Marcus's direction all evening.

Janis watched Roger for a moment. He was a tall man too, well built, with powerful shoulders and thighs, and a loud, cheerful manner. His fair hair was ruffled by the breeze, and his barking laugh drifted across to them. She herself had always found his enthusiasms too relentless, his tastes too strident, but he might have a powerful appeal, she thought now, for a woman who liked her men to be a little larger than life-size. And Emily was so very pretty, in her carefully posed, actressy way, that it was no wonder that Roger was attracted to her.

Roger moved as Janis watched, and went over to the cassette player. Louise cupped her hands. 'Something to dance to,' she shouted.

'You can't dance on the beach,' Janis murmured.

'Course you can. In a shuffly kind of way.'

'Never heard of the sand dance?' Bruce asked, getting to his feet as an old Beatles record blared across the beach. 'Well, this is the shingle dance.' He did a sort of sideways shuffle to *The Octopus's Garden*, slid down a slope of pebbles, and landed on his backside, with his feet up in the air. Louise, laughing, ran to pull him upright.

A few other couples were also jigging and jiving around in the dim light. 'Want to dance?' Marcus asked.

'Shouldn't you go and dance with Emily?'

'Whatever for?' He sounded genuinely surprised at

the idea. 'She's fine. Forget her.' Unexpectedly he moved, trapping Janis beneath him on the shingle, and bending to kiss her.

He smelled of smoke and seaweed, and his lips tasted of salt and wine. Janis responded, but at the same time she was acutely conscious that Emily was only a few yards away, and that this was Emily's boyfriend who was kissing her, Emily's boyfriend who had his arm round her and his hand in her hair, Emily's boyfriend who was stretching out his long body over hers, his thigh forcing hers apart, his breath hot on her face.

'No, Marcus,' she managed to say.

For a moment, his body stilled above her. Then he bent to kiss her again, his lips hard, his tongue invading her, enticing, demanding. 'Let's go over by the cliff,' he whispered.

Involuntarily, Janis glanced sideways. They were perhaps fifty yards from the base of the cliff. It was too dark now to see into its shadows. As soon as they moved away from the fire and the music, they would be as good as alone. Nobody would see them, nobody would come to look for them—until it was time to go back to Louise's, and she would have to meet Emily's eyes in the blazing light of Louise's red and yellow front room. Then Marcus would leave with Emily, and she would be left alone to face Louise and Bruce's curiosity and sympathy, and to drive back on her own to her mother at White Gates.

'No,' she said, more firmly, pushing Marcus away, and getting unsteadily to her feet.

He stood up, too, and took her hand. 'We'd better dance, then.'

The music had changed again. A new hit single, with a thumping disco beat and a yearning woman's voice singing of love and surrender. 'No,' Janis said, moving determinedly in the direction of the little knot of men and girls who were talking among the remains of the food.

Marcus hesitated for a moment, and then he followed her into the light. She had already launched whole-heartedly into a conversation with Sean and one of his friends and, recognising the rejection in her pose, he moved off to talk to somebody else.

Numb and aching inside, Janis talked on. She laughed loudly at Sean's asinine jokes. She danced with Sean, and with Bruce. She even danced with Roger, while Emily was dancing with Marcus. Meeting Louise's glance, she gave a bright smile; catching Marcus's, she looked away hurriedly. Then she busied herself helping Roger and the others tidy away the remains of the barbecue. She was very quiet on the drive back to Louise's bungalow, and as soon as they reached it she excused herself, pleading a headache, and drove alone back to White Gates.

Janis spent a frantic weekend making up her sample garments. She was so busy that she had no time to consider her feelings about Marcus. She cut, pinned, tacked, sewed, pressed, tried the garment on a tailor's dummy and on her own standard-size-twelve figure, pulled them off again and adapted them until she was sure they were perfect. She leafed through her portfolio repeatedly, and tidied up the sketches she meant to show the buyer. She checked over the whole package, and checked it again, to make sure that everything was in order, and that it would all look efficient and professional.

On Saturday morning, Marcus phoned. She had already asked her mother to tell all callers she was out

—mentioning Marcus by name, in case Elizabeth decided he rated as an exception. Her mother compromised by asking him to phone again after lunch.

After lunch, he phoned again. Janis told him, shortly, that she didn't want to talk to him, and put the phone down.

When he phoned yet again, her mother answered. She came up to Janis's studio with a message that Marcus would be over in half an hour.

Janis took one look at the sea of tissue and crêpe jersey that surrounded her, and dashed downstairs to find the telephone book. She tried the number listed next to 'Anson, MH'—what did the 'H' stand for? she couldn't help wondering. No reply. She tried Anson and Williams. No reply. She tried the factory. Again, no reply. She dashed upstairs again, and took a second look at the studio. There was no way she could hide all the evidence in twenty minutes. She went to her bedroom, changed out of her sewing dungarees, which were covered in clinging snippets of jersey and stray tacking threads, and slipped on jeans and a bright yellow sweater with a high front and a deep V at the back. She brushed her hair thoroughly, in case there were any threads caught in that. And, as a final precaution, she locked the studio door and pushed the key to the very back of her dressing-table drawer.

By the time Marcus arrived, she was at the bottom of the garden, and there was a reasonably convincing pile of weeds by her side. She walked over to throw them on the compost heap as he approached, hoping he would taking this for evidence of continuing industry. Then she went to meet him half-way down the lawn, where they would be very clearly in view of her mother, standing on the terrace.

He took her in his arms anyway, to her fury and embarrassment, and attempted to kiss her. She swung her face determinedly away, and snapped loudly, 'Let me go!'

'Not till you've given me a chance to explain.'

'There's nothing to explain.' Janis managed to work herself free. 'It's none of my business,' she said over her shoulder, picking up a trowel again, 'if you go out with Emily. It's nothing to do with me.'

Marcus squatted down on the grass by her side, as she doggedly stuck the trowel into the flowerbed. 'It wasn't how it looked at all.'

Janis turned to him. 'And how,' she said contemptuously, 'do you imagine it looked? To Louise and Bruce and Peter and Cheryl and the rest? How do you imagine it looked to Emily?'

'Emily wasn't looking at us. She's only interested in Roger.'

Janis didn't reply. She dug up another couple of weeds, and Marcus tried again. 'Honestly,' he said, 'Emily and I are through.'

'I'm hardly surprised.'

'We were through before last night. I only brought her to the barbecue because she wanted a chance to see Roger.'

'You can't seriously expect me to believe that,' Janis shot back at him.

Marcus got to his feet, in a flurry of annoyance. 'You never believe anything half-decent of me, do you?'

'I've never had cause to, have I?'

He glared at her, and she glared back at him. His eyes held hers for a long moment. Finally, Janis let her gaze slip.

'I'm sorry,' she murmured. 'That wasn't fair of me.'

'No, it wasn't.' He said it acidly, then relented, and slipped down next to her. 'Can I help?'

Janis hesitated. 'I've done enough for today,' she said. 'Come inside, I'll make you some coffee.'

There was a ladder, Marcus explained, at the squash club. A special kind of league table, up which you climbed and down which you fell by playing the people immediately above or below you.

'You're moving up?' Janis asked.

Marcus shrugged. 'Slowly. New members start at the bottom, of course, and they move up pretty fast till they find their own level. When you've found it, you move a little, but not so much, generally.'

'So you play the same people, a lot of the time?'

'Quite a lot. There was an age, oh, nearly a year, when Bruce was just below me on the ladder. He dropped down a rung or two sometimes, but he never managed to beat me. We must have played a couple of dozen times.'

'That's rough for Bruce—never beating you.'

'He didn't mind so much, he was winning other matches. It may sound a weird system, but squash is one game where you can only have a really good match with someone at pretty much the same standard as yourself. It's a much better arrangement than playing with your mates all the time.'

Janis nodded. It surprised her, how expansive Marcus had become over coffee. She had barely seen him away from work before, with his friends, relaxing and having fun, and he seemed a different man. Younger, less intense.

'So you play a couple of times a week?' she ventured.

'There's always the local league on Tuesdays, and

then we fit in the ladder matches whenever we can make it. Not every week, sometimes it's quite a while before I can agree a date with someone. I'm playing Thursday next week. So I've got Monday free . . .'

'That's my evening-class night,' Janis said quickly.

'How about Wednesday, then? There's the new Spielberg film at the Odeon.'

Janis gulped. She had expected him to ask her out, and she could probably manage Wednesday. It was just after the meeting with the Vane's buyer, so there would be a little less pressure on her then. But one date would lead to others, and soon she'd find her private work schedule slipping seriously behind.

'I usually go swimming on Wednesday,' she said.

'At the baths? I'll leave you to it. Maybe we can fix something up for the weekend, instead.'

'Maybe.' Janis stood up, and carried her empty cup over to the sink. She let it clatter into the washing-up bowl, apprehensive now about her wasted afternoon and her threatened plans.

Marcus caught her mood. 'I must be going,' he said. 'I wanted to get into town before the shops shut. See you at work on Monday?'

'Yes. See you then.'

By Monday morning, Janis was even more apprehensive, and tired: she had worked till late Sunday night on the samples. She had reminded herself of all the reasons she had to mistrust Marcus, and had tried to stop thinking about how much she had enjoyed his company. If necessary, she told herself, she would turn down every date he suggested. It would be better, though, if she could keep him from suggesting any.

She made sure, that day, that the two of them were never alone together. She arrived late at the factory, and left early. Whenever Anthea went to the cloakroom, she found an excuse to go to the workroom. Whenever Marcus showed any signs of hoping to talk to her, she promptly picked up the telephone. From his expression, she could tell that he was puzzled by her behaviour, but he didn't press her, and after a while he began to ignore her in return.

Monday evening was Janis's accountancy class. She went along dutifully, and sat her way through an unbelievably tedious lecture on balance sheets. Maybe some accountants could make people interested in their subject, she thought ruefully, but her lecturer certainly wasn't one of them. She skipped the usual drink in the pub with the rest of the class, and rushed home to put the finishing touches to her package.

On Tuesday, she got up very early, and dressed carefully in one of her own outfits, a low-waisted blue jersey dress with loose sleeves gathered into tight cuffs. She put on her make-up with a care that even Emily would have admired. She polished her shoes and her best red leather handbag. Then she loaded her dress boxes and her portfolio into the back of the Mini, and set off for London.

The Vane's buyer was a girl only a couple of years older than Janis; slim and stylish, full of enthusiasm for bringing new styles into the rather staid stores she worked for. They went all through the portfolio twice, and Janis modelled the samples while the buyer fingered the materials and discussed weights and shades, sizes, costs and production schedules. She shook her head over the fawns and greys, and Janis silently cheered. She loved the wrapover jacket, admired Janis's designs for simple loose-cut tops in lively colours, frowned over the duller shirtdresses and blouses. Janis left with a rush order for a dozen samples of each of three different designs, to go into the Vane's Oxford Street store, and a promise that, if they sold well, there would be big orders to follow.

When she reached the pavement, she couldn't help letting out a whoop of joy. She danced all the way down the street, and even managed a laugh when she saw a parking ticket tucked under her windscreen wiper.

By three o'clock she was back in Smithbury, and in her hairdressers. She was so euphoric that she let Anton have a free hand with her hair, and she emerged with a short, sharp, shiny cut that made her feel young, heartfree and light-headed.

Half-way home, she stopped the car. She went for a walk in the park, and tried to work herself into a frame of mind to face her mother.

She couldn't afford to be euphoric, she knew. She dared not tell her mother about the sample contract, or about the work she was doing behind Marcus's back. She needed to calm down; but that was not all she needed. Somehow, she had to resign her mother to the fact that she would be seeing no more of Marcus.

She couldn't see him, at least for two weeks. She would need every spare evening to work on the samples; and Marcus was not the kind of man who would accept a two-week brush-off, with no explanations given, and then ask her out again. Anyway, there might be other orders from other buyers, and then the two weeks would lengthen into months.

Janis would be sorry about that herself. She dared not admit to herself that she would be more than sorry. But she understood her own motives, and knew that she was making a necessary sacrifice. Elizabeth Trench would not understand, she couldn't be made to understand about the secret contracts and the need to deceive Marcus.

Elizabeth must not be put in a situation where she would think Marcus hard done by, where she might contact him behind Janis's back and scheme to help him win her back. That would give Marcus the perfect opportunity to learn all the things that Janis had so determinedly kept from him. In fact, Janis thought, Elizabeth would probably tell him straight out about the quick change and the locked studio door and the sample tops and jackets and all the rest.

So Elizabeth would have to be made to think that Marcus was in the wrong. It would be dangerous, Janis thought to herself, if she used work as her excuse. Fortunately, there was another excuse readily to hand. She would just have to use Emily. Emily of the false eyelashes, the nail varnish and the streaked blonde hair. Jealousy of Emily would certainly make sense to her mother. It would make enough sense, Janis hoped, to explain all her behaviour to Marcus on Saturday, and her behaviour for the next two weeks.

Two weeks. That was all it needed. Well, say six weeks: two to produce the samples, and another four to see how they sold. In six weeks—two months, at the very outside—she might have a big contract from Vane's to wave in Marcus Anson's face. And then he could be as angry as he liked, but Trenco would be safe, Trenco would be hers, and there would be nothing, nothing at all, that Marcus Anson could do about it!'

CHAPTER SIX

'WHAT on earth,' said Marcus, 'have you done to your hair?'

Janis put a hand to her head, self-consciously. 'I had it cut yesterday,' she said. 'Nice, isn't it?'

'Lovely,' Anthea agreed, behind her back.

'No, it's too short. I like it longer at the sides, like it was before.'

Janis fixed him with the coolest look she could manage. 'I suppose you'll say next,' she said sweetly, 'that you can't stand my clothes, either.'

She'd been asking for it, she knew, but it was still painful to have him look her over in that frank, appraising kind of way.

'They're fine,' he said at last. 'I always like the things you wear. It's only the clothes you design that I can't stomach.'

'How strange. Because this is one of my outfits. Part of my new autumn collection.'

Anthea exploded, and then turned speedily to her typewriter. 'That isn't one of the designs I saw in your studio,' Marcus said.

'True. The ones you saw were the conventional stuff, most of them. This is one of the weird, way-out, hopelessly unwearable designs. I'll show you the sketches I did for it, if you like.'

'Great,' Marcus said. 'You can take me up to your studio tonight.'

She'd been asking for some kind of come-back, she

knew; and it had to be a verbal attack, since Anthea
was there. It still caught her off guard, the way
Marcus always did seem to. A flush came over her
face, before she recovered enough to say, 'Not a hope,
darling. I'll bring the sketches in for you on Friday.'

'I shan't be in on Friday. Sorry, but I've a backlog
of work at the office, and I can only manage one and a
half days this week. We really must have a session
with the computer this morning, so I can show you
some of the entry routines. You'll need to do the input
when I'm not here.'

Janis framed a retort, and then bit it back. She knew
she would have to master the computer properly some
time, if she ever wanted to see Marcus Anson walk out
of Trenco's main door for the last time. What better
time than this, when they were daggers drawn, and
when she had her secret knowledge of the new
contract to buoy her up?

'As soon as I've had a cup of coffee,' she said lightly,
'to warm me up a bit.'

'Feeling chilly around the ears, are you?'

Anthea went over to put the kettle on, and Janis
glanced up at her, suddenly concerned. She knew
Anthea wasn't exactly indifferent to Marcus, either.
Surely Anthea had noticed that things between Janis
and Marcus had changed, that in spite of all the gibes
and spats it was no longer Marcus and Anthea against
Janis but, in some strange way, Marcus and Janis,
indissolubly tied together? If she was in the other
girl's position, she knew, she would be unbearably
jealous—perhaps too jealous even to be able to
continue working at Trenco.

Janis watched, intensely aware, as Anthea presented
Marcus with his coffee first, strong and black as he
liked it, and then brought her own over afterwards.

She saw Marcus look up and smile at Anthea. And she saw, to her relief, that the smile Anthea gave in return was bright and cheerful and quite, quite lacking in passion.

Ironically, even that gave her a pang of jealousy. She couldn't imagine there ever being a time when she and Marcus would be able to smile at each other in that easy, light, uncomplicated way. She pulled her chair a little closer to his, suddenly anxious to reassert her claim on him, and leaned forward in concentration as he began to call up the screens of the accounting programs, and explain them to her.

It was difficult to keep concentrating, with Marcus so close by her side. He seemed to be triumphantly aware that he had her captive. He kept giving her little sideways glances, catching her eye, touching her hand with his, even brushing his knee against hers. She was painfully aroused by him, even more so because she knew that now there was even less chance than before that they would ever be lovers. Before too long, Marcus would find out about the sample contract, and then he would know he had lost, and his anger, she suspected, would be enough to utterly dwarf any of the rages she had yet witnessed.

After it, he would surely abandon Trenco. There would be no need for him to keep on then, because Trenco would be safe, and there would be nothing to fear from Mr Jenkins at the bank. There would be no cause for him to keep on, because he would have lost his dream of making the company his own, shaping it as he intended. She would have won her company back, but she would have lost Marcus. Not, she reminded herself bitterly, that she had ever really had him. Except as a bank nominee to the board of Trenco. There he had done a very good job, she had to admit. Even with all the distractions he provided, it was easy for Janis to follow the workings of the new computerised book-keeping system. He went through the balance sheets, and cleared away all the mystery and confusion that the evening-class lecturer had instilled into her mind, making it all seem simple and obvious.

When they had finished this—and when Anthea had gone off to lunch—he took her through the monthly results, showing her how Trenco's finances had declined after her father's death, and how they were slowly, slowly turning the corner, tightening their stock control, improving their budgeting, increasing the margin on the orders they accepted. Of course, the results of these changes took time to show in the figures, and though the graphs of his long-term forecasts all turned reassuringly upwards, some of the lines were currently wavering well below the target levels.

'Marcus——' Janis said slowly.

'Yes, love?'

She chose to ignore that. 'I can see . . . I mean, it's all very clear. Anyone could see what a mess we were in, and how things are improving. But . . . what would happen if Mr Jenkins was to switch on the computer, and take a look at all this? Right now? Tomorrow, say?'

Marcus grinned, and ran a hand through his hair, pushing it back out of his eyes. 'Just how many times,' he asked gently, 'have you taken a look at this system when I've been out of the office?'

Janis flushed. 'Two or three. Well, three or four, actually.'

'How many of these graphs did you take a look at?'

She frowned. 'I don't remember seeing this one

before. In fact, I'm sure I didn't see this one, or the last couple. But then, I didn't know my way around the system, did I? And Mr Jenkins would.'

'Let me show you something else,' Marcus said. He leaned forward, tapped some keys, and she watched him exiting from all the programs, and turning back to a blank computer screen. 'This is how it looked when you switched on?'

Janis nodded.

'Right, find your way back to the overall profit forecast. The one I showed you a couple of minutes ago.'

He moved over just a little, and slid the keyboard towards her. She typed a few commands, checked the screen, typed some more, and some more—and finally stopped, puzzled.

'What did I do wrong?'

Marcus laughed. 'Nothing.'

'But, when I did this for myself, I found that overall forecast with no trouble; and you hadn't explained it all then.'

'You were supposed to. Here, give me the keyboard back a minute.'

He leaned over, reaching a careless arm across her shoulders, and typed rapidly with the other hand. The menu screens that had confounded Janis disappeared. 'Now, try again.'

Janis repeated her commands; and this time, to her confusion, she found the forecast with no trouble. She banged her fist on the edge of the desk in annoyance, and threw herself backwards in her chair.

'OK, Superman, explain it.'

'If you'd been watching carefully, you'd be able to explain it yourself.'

'I can't have been, can I?' There was a nasty,

triumphant glint in Marcus's eye. 'Come on, take pity on me.'

'Since you ask so nicely.' Marcus smiled disarmingly at her. 'It's quite simple. All these program modules are password-protected. They can be locked. It's just like locking a filing cabinet, really, except that it's done with electronic passwords. I've set up three different levels of access to the system. There's the version I showed you first of all: that's the full version, that I use myself. Then there's the version you called up when you sneaked your little looks at the system behind my back. And then there's the version I showed you just now. That's the version we'd show Jenkins, or your mother, if we needed to let them take a look.'

'With different figures.'

Marcus shook his head from side to side. 'Janis, Janis! That would be unethical. No, the same figures, but interpreted differently. Laid out differently, so that it's not so easy to discover our current position from a quick glance. Jenkins would have access to all the ledgers, but not to the graphs which give you that instant check on our financial situation. He'd have access to spreadsheets which cover only the period up to three months ago. Without lying to him, or really misleading him, I could give him the impression that the most recent figures simply weren't on the system yet. I could let him have free access, explore that level as much as he likes, press any key he chooses, and he'd never find those graphs.'

'That's diabolical!'

He laughed. 'I wouldn't put it quite like that. It's . . . well, it's on the edge of acceptability. I wouldn't do the same kind of thing for my regular clients. But we're in a drastic situation still, and I told you I've had to take some drastic steps. In a few months' time, I'll be able to scrap this whole protection system, and show anybody how we're doing without a care in the world. But not yet. Not yet.'

'And what,' Janis persisted, 'about the third system?'

'The one I set up for you? I knew you'd need to check on what I was doing, how things were going. I just thought I'd make it easy for you, by leading you straight to the forecasts. They're the same figures, again, but set out in all their stark awfulness.'

'But I didn't type in any passwords.'

'You didn't need to. I did all that for you.'

Janis stared at him. 'You mean, you trapped me!'

'It wasn't a trap, darling. I've nothing to hide from you.'

'But you knew I was sneaking looks at the system behind your back.'

'Of course I did. You've never pretended to trust me, have you? I thought I might as well make the best of it, save you wasting too much time.'

'So every time you walked out of here, you set the whole damn thing up, just waiting for me to come and check up on you?'

'That's right. I even programmed in a check routine, so I'd know when you'd called the programs up. Four times, actually.'

Janis was still taking in the enormity of this confession when Anthea returned. Marcus rose promptly from his seat. 'Good timing, Anthea. I ought to be going. And now——' he smiled down at Janis '—the boss knows everything.'

Do I? Janis thought, as she watched him ruffle Anthea's curly hair, grab his jacket, and disappear through the door. Do I?

*   *   *

At first, Janis thought of producing the sample garments for Vane's in her studio. There were too many, she soon decided. She needed at least one helper, and there was only one sewing maching in the studio. The whole operation would be on a scale her mother wouldn't be able to help noticing. Though she had dropped some hefty hints to her mother that Marcus had acted abominably and broken her heart, she still didn't want to let Elizabeth Trench think that she was doing work behind his back. The temptation her mother would feel to talk to him about it or, even worse, to Mr Jenkins, might prove too great.

The only alternative was to do the work in the factory workshop, in the evenings. She could clear it away, she reckoned, at the end of each session, and hide all the evidence in a big box in the storeroom, where Marcus—as far as she knew—rarely ventured. She already knew who she would choose to help her. Stella's husband still had not found a new job, and she was pathetically grateful when Janis offered her the extra work at time-and-a-half's pay.

The pay had to come out of Janis's own pocket, since Marcus had such a tight control of Trenco's finances, and she borrowed some money on her credit card to enable her to cover this without raising any suspicions at the bank. The same source bought her the materials she needed. She typed out the contract with Vane's herself, two-fingered, after Anthea had left the office.

The risk she was running, this time, was that Marcus too might choose to return one evening, to do some work on the accounts. If he did, there would be absolutely no opportunity to hide the evidence of what she was up to. In any case, she was aware that it was only a matter of time before he discovered it. But the longer she could spin it out, the closer she could get to a fat contract for her designs, the more certain her victory over him would be.

He didn't come that night, or Thursday night, or Friday. She had already warned Stella that he might, and that if there were any arguments Stella was to leave fast, and let her sort out Marcus. But he didn't come, and Janis had to admit that she was vaguely disappointed. There were the sample tops and jackets, sizes ten and twelve and fourteen, the stack of them growing at the back of the storeroom, but the sight of them gave her less pleasure than she had expected. She spent a dull weekend, working mostly, and going for a long walk on her own. Then the next week drifted by in a flurry of work and work and work. Marcus at the office was distant and polite, and Marcus in the evenings—she tried not to think about Marcus in the evenings, when she bent over her sewing machine with Stella.

Tuesday and Thursday she had appointments with more buyers. The Tuesday buyer flicked through her sketches dismissively, and advised her to keep on producing shirts. But the Thursday one loved the bright-coloured tops, and looked carefully at the shirtdresses, and ordered two dozen samples, just to try out, for her chain's Manchester branch. So many firms seemed inflexible on their order dates, she said, but Trenco was so efficient and reliable, and if Janis could produce the samples quickly, and promise to meet a full follow-up order within two months, then that would suit her plans for her new in-store boutique perfectly.

Janis typed out another order confirmation, two-fingered, on Anthea's typewriter, and negotiated another week's overtime with Stella. Stella suggested that Deirdre, who worked next to her, might help too, but Janis checked on her credit-card limit and decided she couldn't afford to pay Deirdre as well. Not yet.

That weekend she went away. The first batch of sample garments were almost finished. She planned to work on them on Sunday night, and on Tuesday night, leaving Monday to her evening class. Then, on Thursday when Marcus was not at Trenco, she would deliver them personally to the Vane's warehouse just outside London. By then, she would have started on the next batch, and there were still three more buyers to see. Victory was coming closer and closer.

It was fun seeing her old friend Jane from college, staying in Jane's chaotic flat in Parson's Green, and going to a party on Saturday night with Jane and her flatmates. She met a surveyor called James at the party, and went to an art exhibition with him on Sunday afternoon. He asked for her phone number, and promised to ring in a week or two, when she might be free to see him. But she came home still curiously low and dissatisfied, as if something vital had gone missing from her life.

She didn't expect to find it again at her evening class on Monday, but she went along anyway, and sat through a lecture of mind-numbing boredom on the intricacies of profit and loss accounts. When the lecture finished, she came out of the college to find that it was pouring with rain. It had been fine when she had left home and, ignoring the black clouds on the horizon, she hadn't brought an umbrella, so she pulled her loose jacket high at her neck, put her head down, and made a run for it, cursing the fact that she'd parked the Mini two streets away.

Just outside the college gate she ran slap bang into somebody. She panted an apology, and was about to run on when she found herself trapped by a strong arm.

'This way,' said Marcus, opening his car door and pushing her gently inside.

It was the green MG, parked on double yellow lines. By the time Janis had shaken the drips from her hair, Marcus had joined her and was driving off.

'I parked my car in Brighton Street,' Janis said helpfully.

'I'll retrieve it for you later.'

'Er . . . where exactly are we going?'

'My flat. It's not far.'

This temporarily silenced her. Somehow, she had still not managed to make an effective protest by the time Marcus turned off the road and into an underground garage.

'I really don't think——' Janis began, as Marcus helped her out of the car.

'There's no need to think. I'll do the thinking for both of us.'

'You arrogant, self-satisfied, offensive, rude, opinionated . . .'

'Man,' Marcus finished for her. He put his arms around her, and kissed her.

'Oh, no,' Janis said weakly, when she had got her breath back.

'Oh, yes,' Marcus said. He pushed back the damp hair from her forehead, and kissed her again. 'This way.'

Somehow, they got from the car to the lift, and from the lift to the door of Marcus's flat, and from there into Marcus's living-room, and Janis had still not protested properly. Marcus shrugged off his wet jacket and came over to her, then began to unfasten hers, slowly, button by button. When it hung loose, he slipped his hands underneath it, and cupped her breasts through her thin sweater.

A little tremor ran through her. Marcus's eyes, fixed on hers, were wide and dark, and on his face was an expression, not of triumph, but of uncertainty and determination, queerly mixed. He pulled her to him, very gently, and she came, and put her arms around his shoulders. Her breasts were alive and aching from his touch, the nipples hard buds of awareness as she pressed tightly against his chest. She could feel his hands drawing her sweater up at the back and running over the bare skin beneath, cool, caressing. His tongue traced her jawline, his teeth dug gently into the little hollow under her jawbone and then nipped a path down the tendons of her neck.

Janis let out a little moan, blind now to everything but the intensity of her desire for him. And Marcus, moving his hands, suddenly picked her up in his arms and carried her across the room, shouldering open a door and depositing her, very gently, in the middle of a wide bed.

He stood there for a moment, by the bed, looking down at her, almost as if he was offering her a chance to resist. Then he sat on the side of the bed, and reached out to her. He pulled her towards him, and drew her sweater up and over her head. He reached down to the zip of her skirt, and helped her to slide out of it, peeled her tights gently down from her waist and off her legs.

As his mouth claimed hers again, Janis wrapped her bare legs around him, aching to have him closer, aching to feel his bare flesh against hers, and reached out to unfasten his shirt.

'Slowly,' Marcus whispered, his breath warm against her face. 'Not yet. Slowly.'

His mouth drifted down and across her body with agonising slowness, possessing, arousing every square inch of her skin. He pushed aside the lacy cup of her bra, and his tongue circled tantalisingly around her breast, teasing, caressing, bringing her to a painful peak of longing. Then it moved to her other breast, and he reached to unfasten her bra and explore the swelling lower slopes. His teeth closed gently around her nipple, his rough chin rasped against her tender skin. His hand traced a path down her stomach, and moved, lightly, tauntingly, across the sensitive skin of her inner thighs. When she stirred, shaken by unbearable waves of longing, his body stilled her, urging her to match his control, to savour this last agonising pleasure of waiting. She pushed her hands through the short, rough hair at the back of his neck, and listened to his breathing, fast and ragged, as he tore away at the last shreds of his own self-control.

When Janis was certain she could endure it no longer, he drew away from her, and began to undress, slowly, unhurriedly. He shrugged off his shirt, stood to unfasten his trousers. She lay back on his bed, luxuriating in the delight of watching him and yet impatient for the infinitely greater delight of feeling him flesh to flesh with her. Naked, he was lean and muscular, with an arrogant, efficient power to him, and an aggressive masculinity that made her draw in her breath in a thrilling mixture of desire and apprehension.

He measured his length against hers, lowered his weight gently on to her, kissed her again, deeply, demandingly, as his body spelled out its own message of longing and delight. Her skin felt raw where his touched it; she was overwhelmed by the sensations he gave her. She arched her body up against his, aching to feel every part of him. His hands moved behind her, drawing her still closer, and his thigh slid between hers, hard and male and unfamiliar.

After a few moments he moved, drawing gently apart from her. He fell on to his back next to her, and then propped himself up on an elbow, and looked over at her. Looking back at him, Janis felt curiously vulnerable.

'You should have told me you were a virgin.'

He did not sound angry, but surprised—offended, almost.

'I didn't know how to.'

'I'd have been more gentle if I'd known.'

She gave him a wavery smile, 'I didn't want you to be more gentle.'

'Oh, Janis.' He bent and kissed her again, lightly. 'Are you still trying to fight me?'

She didn't answer him.

'Are you mad at me?' He ran a cool finger across her forehead. 'I know I shouldn't have done that. But I thought I'd never get you any other way.'

No, she thought to herself. No, you'd never have got me any other way.

Marcus waited a moment for the answer that didn't come, and then stood up. 'I'll make some coffee,' he said, reaching for a towelling robe that hung behind the bedroom door. 'The bathroom's through there.'

Janis lay there for a little while longer after he'd disappeared, and then got up and went through to the bathroom. It was Marcus-like: neat, slightly austere, totally masculine. Her body felt soft and strange to her, and she washed quickly, almost guiltily. There was another bathrobe behind the door, and she put that on, conscious that he had worn it, of the faint Marcus smell that came from it.

Marcus was in the bedroom when she came back, picking up her clothes and his from the floor. A tray of coffee stood on a low table by the bed. She took in the details of the room for the first time: the straight modern lines of the furniture, the white walls and dark blue bedspread, the huge windows, undraped, black, reflecting the two of them.

'These are damp,' he said critically, feeling her sweater and skirt. 'You can't wear them tonight. I'll lend you some clothes to go home in.'

She stood watching him, tongue-tied, and he came across and put his hands on her shoulders. 'Would you like that?' He grinned at her, and her heart melted painfully inside her. 'Wearing my clothes?'

'They wouldn't fit.'

'That'd be half the fun.'

'What would my mother think?'

'She won't stay up, will she, if you're late home?'

'Is it late?' Janis glanced down, and found she was still wearing her watch. It was barely ten-thirty, just an hour and a half since she had come from her evening class.

'No, but you're not going yet.' He felt her body stiffen under his hands, and pulled her back down on the bed. 'Oh, no, you're not. If you go now, you might manage to persuade yourself you hate me by the morning. And if you stay, I'll be able to convince you that you don't.'

His eyes looked for hers, and she tried to avoid them. But he brought his hands to her head, trapping it, drawing her round to face him, and she couldn't hide from him any longer. He held her gaze for a long moment, his eyes black and liquid, wide open to her, and then he bent and kissed her again. His lips lingered, gentle and persuasive, against hers. Hers wavered and then parted under the light, insistent pressure, and his tongue snaked into her mouth, triumphantly reasserting his possession of her.

'Marcus. Marcus, please let me go.' He was already unfastening the belt of the bathrobe, reaching under it, reclaiming her body.

Marcus shook his head. He took her hand, bent to kiss her wrist, and then pulled it towards him, leading her to discover his resurgent arousal. She trembled, and his hand tightened round hers, curling her fingers around him, strong and determined and not gentle at all. 'It's always better,' he whispered, 'the second time.'

Amazingly, it had been, Janis thought to herself as she drove home alone in Marcus's green MG. He'd wanted to drive her home, but she had refused insistently, worried enough already about what her mother would say, and they had compromised on this. He had promised to retrieve her car in the morning, and drive it himself to Trenco.

She was wearing an old shirt of Marcus's, a loud checked flannel shirt that drooped from her shoulders and bagged around her waist, and a pair of his jeans that she'd had to turn half-way up her legs. There was something very erotic about the feel of his old clothes on her slim body, about the harsh rub of the fabric against her glowing skin. She felt luminous with delight, weak with the memory of their lovemaking.

It had been more abandoned the second time, slower, less urgent, with Marcus exploring her body in ways she had never though she would permit to any man, carrying her beyond doubt and shame, forcing her to express her delight in each caress, making her cry out for more. He had urged her to make love to him in return, to feel and touch and taste every inch of him, until she felt she knew his body almost better than she knew her own. She had gloried in him as he had gloried in her, laughing, kissing, loving, aching with pleasure, forced to confront her sexual nature openly and to take a keen delight in it.

For an evening they had belonged to each other totally. She had opened herself to him in ways in which she had never opened herself to any human being before. And yet tomorrow they would be back at the factory, to their private battle for control of Trenco. Tomorrow all the doubt and suspicion, all the secrets would be back with them. Tomorrow, Janis knew with painful certainty, Marcus would be her enemy once again.

CHAPTER SEVEN

JANIS was late to work in the morning. Her yellow Mini was neatly parked in its usual spot when she manoeuvred the MG—an unpredictable beast, as she had always feared, with a mind of its own when it came to steering and acceleration—along next to it. She gave a last glance around the clean, shabby interior, with all its tiny reminders of Marcus, and weighed the keys in her hand as she stepped out. His shirt and jeans were neatly folded in the boot. She had carried them stealthily downstairs, wrapped in an old Sainsbury's carrier bag, while her mother was busy with the washing up. She still held in her mind the uncomfortable reminder of her mother peeping out of the dining-room window to wave goodbye to her, and taking in the unfamiliar car, open-mouthed. She had till six o'clock to think of a convincing explanation.

And she had precisely ten seconds to think how she was going to greet Marcus: except that there was no possible way to greet him, expecially with Anthea there. She quickened her step as she made for the factory door, determined to get the agony over, the keys jingling incriminatingly in her hand.

'You're late,' he said as she came into the office.

'I had to go to the doctor's.' That had been the first of the day's unpleasant tasks, though it hadn't been as ghastly as she had feared. Dr Brown had been brisk and businesslike, totally unsurprised, not at all critical.

Marcus nodded. 'A sore throat,' Janis added, for Anthea's benefit.

Anthea brought over her coffee. 'Funny,' she said, 'you look really well this morning. Glowing with health.'

'Radiant,' Marcus agreed.

Janis shot him a poisonous look. 'Must be the effect of the medicine,' she said.

'Take it gently,' Marcus said, 'if you're not feeling too good.'

He reached out his hand, and squeezed hers. Janis pulled herself free, and dashed across the office to bury her face in the filing cabinets before Anthea noticed how scarlet it had become.

'Anthea,' Marcus went on, 'could you be a love and take this letter to the post box for me? I want you to make sure it catches the first post.'

Anthea opened her mouth to protest, then saw his warning expression, and made a rapid departure. Janis, face to the wall, heard Marcus's footsteps coming across the office towards her.

'Kiss me now,' he said quietly, 'and I promise to behave myself for the rest of the day.'

His hands were already drawing her round, before she could refuse, and then his mouth was on hers, and all the glorious feelings of the night before came rushing back in a torrent. She clung to him for a moment, unsteadily, and then pushed herself away. He looked so much like the Marcus of the office, the enemy Marcus, in his dark suit and grey shirt, and yet he felt and acted so much like the Marcus of the previous night. When he smiled at her, his face alive with happiness, she couldn't help smiling back and reaching out again to reassure herself that he was real.

'This must be appallingly obvious to Anthea.'

'It must,' he agreed.

'How embarrassing!'

He grinned. 'Don't worry, Janis. People are always nice to lovers. It's a well known fact.'

Lovers, thought Janis. Marcus and I are lovers. I love him, yet I still can't trust him. And when he discovers what I've been doing on the design contracts . . . it's all so sure to fall to pieces. Oh, my gosh, if it's hard to face Anthea now, how is it going to be facing Anthea then, when Marcus walks out on me in fury? Her lip trembled, and Marcus, mistaking her thoughts, stilled it with another kiss.

'You'll want your car keys back,' said Janis, struggling to return the morning to normality.

'And yours.' He reached in his pocket for them. 'It's misfiring a little, the engine needs adjusting. I'll come round this evening and take a look at it for you.'

This evening. Janis froze. That evening she would be finishing off the samples for Vane's, with Stella. And Marcus would expect to see her! She had given him every reason to think she wanted him to be with her, to spend his free time with her—and she had no free time, because it all had to be spent on the samples. If she confessed that, Marcus would be furious, and stalk off, and—oh, she couldn't bear it!

'I'm—I've already arranged to go out this evening, Marcus.' She walked back to her desk and sat down, hoping desperately that Anthea would come back quickly.

Marcus gave her a long, thoughtful look. 'Let me know when you're free, then,' he said softly.

'Maybe Wednesday.'

'Maybe?' His voice was hurt, accusing. Then he forced a smile. 'I guess I can survive till Wednesday,' he said lightly, and bent to kiss her head before he

went to sit back at his own desk. When Anthea
reappeared a moment later, they were hard at work,
side by side, as if nothing at all had changed.

Marcus left first that evening. Anthea glanced over at
Janis when he was gone, as if she was hoping for confessions, but Janis's baleful stare must have convinced
her she was on the wrong track, and she went herself a
moment afterwards. Janis stayed for a few minutes in
the empty office, looking around.

It had all changed so much since Marcus had come.
All the old things were still there, Anthea's geraniums
and her Cézanne prints on the walls and the filing
cabinets and the order books. His desk and computer
only took up one corner. But somehow everything in
the office bore Marcus's stamp, as if the sheer power
of his personality had brought him to dominate them
all. She herself bore Marcus's stamp now. Taken and
branded and possessed: Marcus Anson's woman.
Until he realised that she had not really submitted to
him at all, that she had been fighting to regain her
own control over her life—and that she was on the
verge of winning.

She clenched her hands on the side of her desk. She
would have to see him on Wednesday, or he would
suspect something. Perhaps she could go back to the
office late, and start on some of the new batch of
samples after she had left him. Then on Thursday she
would deliver to Vane's, and Thursday evening she
could maybe get to the factory, and Friday . . . What if
he wanted to see her on Friday? And, if the next
buyers she saw gave her orders, what could she say to
them? And how would she find the time to do the
work, and the money to pay Stella, and . . .

She could keep it up for maybe another week, she

decided, long enough to complete the order she had already taken on. She could pay Deirdre to do some of the work so she would have more time to spend with Marcus. Well, she couldn't actually pay Deirdre, but she could promise to pay Dierdre as soon as the money for the first samples came through. Then she would deliver that order, and then . . . Then there would be no alternative. She would have to tell Marcus.

It wasn't long enough. There wouldn't be time for the Vane's buyer to discover how the samples were selling. She would almost certainly not have a big order by then. If she told Marcus before she had signed a big order, she believed he might veto any orders that she subsequently won. Perhaps she should cancel the second order, and throw all her hopes behind Vane's and the first sample run.

But she had already signed the second order, and it was unprofessional to pull out. Perhaps she could borrow some more money, and fulfil the two orders without telling Marcus yet? There would be no risk to it, because she would certainly be paid for those garments, even if no further orders followed.

Janis frowned. She would have used up every last penny of her own credit by the time she had paid Stella that week's overtime. It was out of the question to borrow from her mother. She couldn't possibly talk to the bank. It would be too risky to go to another bank, impossible to explain to them why she wanted the loan. Who else did she know with money? Certainly, not her brother. Louise? Louise and Bruce were not exactly flush with money, but Louise surely had a credit card.

That was the only answer. She would have to visit Louise early that evening, beg for help, and then come later to the factory to work with Stella. It was a mess—but it might work.

She locked up the empty factory, and wandered outside in a haze of conflicting plans and ideas. She had started her car and put it into reverse before she noticed there was a note taped on the steering wheel. With her feet pressed down hard on the pedals, she reached to rip it off.

'I love you. M.'

The car spluttered and coughed, complained and died as Janis collapsed over the wheel, the tears flooding down her face and streaking down the little note across Marcus's angular writing.

'This sounds to me,' said Louise, 'like another occasion for the cooking brandy.'

She put down her paintbrush and went to the sink. From the front room, they coud hear faint gunshots coming from the television. Bruce was watching a western.

'Thanks,' said Janis, taking a cautious sip.

'I take it the problem is Marcus.'

Janis nodded.

'Are you pregnant?'

'Oh, no! Heavens, no! I mean—no.'

'I get the message. Sorry for asking. I just had the impression things were . . .'

'They are,' Janis confessed. 'But that's not the problem.'

'A crisis at work?'

Janis nodded.

'Well, if things are—however they are—between you and Marcus, why don't you let him sort it out?'

'Because he'd do it all wrong. He'd cancel my contract.

He'd blow his top and walk out. I mean, he's going to do that anyway, but I want to get my contract first.'

Louise eyed her, amused and concerned. She picked up the paintbrush and put it in a pot of water to soak. She sat down again with her glass of cooking brandy and said, 'I think you'd better start at the start.'

Janis started at the start. Half an hour later, when she had got as far as Louise's credit card, Louise got up, walked to the door, and shouted into the front room, 'Bruce!'

'Oh, no!' Janis cried.

Louise swung round, a determined look on her face. 'Janis,' she said, 'if you want to mess around with loans behind Marcus's back, that's your problem, but I don't do things behind Bruce's back. If you borrow my money, you borrow our money. Understood?'

Janis gulped. 'Understood.'

'Now, you'd better repeat that—all of it, right from the start—to Bruce.'

An hour later, Janis was driving to the factory, with the memory of a very uncomfortable argument behind her, and with Louise and Bruce's promise of a loan to tide her over for a month. Only a month, they had insisted, and only on condition that she promise to come clean to Marcus when the month was up.

They had both been adamant that she was being totally unfair to Marcus, that she was wrong to keep him in the dark, and that it was absolutely inconceivable that he would cancel her contracts. Janis knew how wrong they were. Maybe to Bruce, Marcus was the nice guy he played squash with; but to Janis, a large part of Marcus was still the iron-willed accountant who had demanded that she follow his policies for Trenco, and who would, she knew, be absolutely furious when he learned how persistently she had disobeyed him.

And the other part of Marcus, the part that had made love to her the night before, the part that had written 'I love you'—that part had to be lived with, somehow, for the next month. Without letting him suspect what she was doing.

Stella looked up from the cutting table as Janis came into the workshop. 'This is the last batch,' she said cheerfully.

'It'll need to be. I won't be able to work on the order tomorrow, so it'll all need to be packed up tonight.'

'We should manage that.'

'Let's get going.' Janis went to switch on the kettle, then grabbed a pair of scissors, and set to work.

Two hours later, they were pressing the last seam. Janis sighed. Turning out one-off samples, changing size and colour after every couple of garments, was so much more time-consuming than the regular shirt production. She had done a very rough-and-ready run through Marcus's costing program—carefully erasing all trace of her work from the computer afterwards—and knew that, however optimistically she costed them, and even without allowing for her own time, these sample contracts would not make a penny profit. But they were the start, the way ahead for Trenco, and it would all be worth it in the end.

'I'll stack these in the car boot,' she started to say, and then stopped to think. Marcus might take a look at the Mini the following evening; it was too great a risk. She would have to come into the factory very early on Thursday morning, and load the garments then.

Elizabeth Trench smiled to herself. From her bedroom window, she could look out on to the drive of White Gates. She could see Janis's yellow Mini parked just outside the garage, with the bonnet lifted, and two jean-clad figures leaning inside. As she watched, they both straightened up, and two dark heads moved close together, and then a little apart. They seemed to be wrestling over a spanner. But they had kissed too, surely, when they'd moved together, and that was a comforting sign.

It wasn't at all like it had been in her young days, she couldn't help thinking, when young men arrived for dates in smart suits and only kissed you on the doorstep at the end of the evening. She really couldn't understand what had been going on between Janis and Marcus these past few weeks. At least it was a sign of normality, though, that he should have called at the house in the evening and taken her out to dinner. And whatever Janis had been up to on Monday—Elizabeth didn't like to make too serious an attempt to fit the pieces together, since she had a sneaking feeling that she wouldn't like the answer very much—it had made her eyes shine and her skin glow, and—well, there was no doubt about it, Janis was in love. Which was exactly what her mother had been wanting to see.

She watched Janis get into the car and start it, and lean out of the window, saying something to Marcus and laughing; she watched Marcus slam down the bonnet and go to join her in the other front seat. She heard the Mini roar off down Roselea Crescent. When, some time later, she heard it roaring back, and heard two pairs of footsteps making their way up, past her bedroom and towards Janis's attic studio, she decided it would be wiser, much wiser, if she pretended to have gone to bed early, and not to have noticed a thing.

*　　*　　*

Marcus roamed around the studio. He peered critically at the sketch pinned on to Janis's easel. He leafed through her portfolio, holding up some of the drawings to the light, frowning slightly at one or two of them. He opened drawers and peeped inside. He looked at the sewing machine, at the iron and ironing board, at Janis's overflowing boxes of threads and pins and buttons. He ran a finger down the blade of her cutting scissors. He drifted across to the pair of shirtdresses that hung on hangers from hooks on a low rafter, and fingered their folds.

Janis, leaning against the sill of the dormer window, watched him. He was not paying any attention to her, but she knew that he was conscious of her presence, that he would never have nosed around in this shameless way if she hadn't been there with him.

It was a strange sensation, seeing him here in her private sanctuary. There was the pleasure of watching him, of seeing the dark hair falling forwards on to his face, the way his well worn jeans clung to his hips and thighs, the occasional hint of a smile at the corners of his mouth. She thought there might have been a certain annoyance, at the same time, in seeing him invade her territory so shamelessly. But it felt much as it had two nights before, when he had gazed down at her naked body. There was nothing to be ashamed of here, nothing she did not want him to see, to touch, to take pleasure in. Mind, that was only because she had had the chance to hide at the factory all the things he was not to see . . .

He opened the drawer at the end of the old kitchen table, the one where she used to keep the spare key to the factory.

'It's not here,' he said, glancing across at her for the first time in ten minutes or more.

Janis smiled. 'The key? you have it, you idiot.'

'I thought you might have had another one made.'
She shook her head.

Marcus pushed the portfolio to one side, and sat down on the table in the space he had cleared. He glanced around again.

'Does your mother ever come up here?'

'Not often. She sometimes brings me a cup of coffee while I'm working. She sweeps the floor and dusts, she insists on that. But she never cleans up the table or the easel or anything. She knows I hate people to mess with my things.'

He grinned at her, teasing. 'I thought you'd stop me sooner.'

'On Monday?' Janis reddened, wondering suddenly if he really had expected her to protest, to fight, to stop him before they reached his bedroom.

'I really meant tonight.' He reached out a hand, and she crossed to him hesitantly. He opened his legs and she stood between them, in the V of his thighs. He pulled her close and crossed his ankles behind her, trapping her. Seated, his face was almost level with hers. 'Though it's the same thing, in a way. You protect your space so fiercely, you hate people to invade you, to threaten your privacy. You squirm, usually, if anyone touches you unexpectedly or looks at your work when you're not ready to show them it. But, when I did break through those strong defences of yours, you suddenly seemed to have no resistance left. You let me take you just as I wanted, every way I wanted on Monday. And tonight you stood there, watching me look at all your drawings, hunt through your cupboards, open your drawers, without ever once saying "Don't" or "Not there" or "That's private" to me.'

Her head was turned down, and she didn't answer. After a moment, Marcus reached out a hand to tilt her chin and make her look at him. She couldn't hide, then, the tears that were running down her face.

'Janis! Darling!' His arms went round her, pulling her still tighter, drawing her head on to his shoulder. 'Darling, I didn't mean to criticise. I love it in you, your openness. I love knowing that you've let me share what you've hidden from the rest of the world. You can do the same with me. Everything of mine is yours to explore—I've no secrets from you.'

Her fingers clenched on his shoulder and upper arm, and the sobs intensified. She took in great gulps of air, fighting to regain control of herself. Marcus's voice was low and steady, his words were reassuring, his touch firm against her, but she was conscious of a slight undercurrent of annoyance, as if he found her outburst embarrassing, and more conscious that he had not the remotest idea why she was really crying, and that she could not possibly tell him.

'That's better,' he said, as she swallowed the last of the sobs, and began to breathe more steadily. 'Hey, will you do something for me?'

'What?'

'Put on that dress? The green one, hanging up. It does fit you?'

She smiled, unsteadily. 'Of course it does. I always make up the designs in my own size.'

'I want to see you wearing it.'

'OK.'

She peeled off the jeans and sweater she had worn to work on the car, conscious that he really wanted, not see her in the dress, but to have her strip in front of him. He watched her intently as she walked across the studio, dressed only in bra and pants, and slipped the green dress over her shoulders. It was a pretty colour, but the design, she knew, had not been much of a success. The dresses in the studio were both designs the buyers had rejected, while all the samples of the clothes she was making for them were safely locked away in the factory storeroom.

She couldn't reveal her dissatisfaction with the dress to Marcus, though, and she hoped that he'd think any uneasiness she showed simply reflected her feeling that she didn't look her best with the tearstains on her face.

Not that he seemed to notice. 'You're so beautiful,' he whispered, slipping off the table and coming across to where she stood in the centre of the room.

'Marcus, we can't . . .' she murmured, when his mouth released hers.

'Can't what?' he teased, in an undertone. 'Can we go to your room?'

'My bedroom? Heavens, no! It's opposite my mother's.'

'And she's in bed?'

'She must be. It's awfully late.'

'She won't come in here, then, will she?'

He was already unbuttoning the green dress again, intent, determined.

'No, but darling, we can't . . .'

'Can't make love here? Of course we can. Lock the door if you're worried.'

When Janis hesitated, he went to lock it for her. The key was already in the lock, and he slipped it into his pocket. A little thrill went through Janis. Herself and Marcus, shut in the studio together.

It was so different from the time before. Everything was different except for the feel of his body, the look in his dark eyes as they met hers, the surge of joy as they joined together.

'Can't?' he teased. 'Can't? I'll show you what we can do . . .'

The studio would never seem quite the same again. Nor would it ever be exactly the same again, Janis thought the next morning, as she peeped in briefly and rediscovered the chaos she and Marcus had wreaked as they had made love. The key was still in the pocket of his jeans, and she shut the door firmly, cursing the fact that she'd forgotten about it, and praying that her mother wouldn't feel the urge to dust that day. 'Can't . . .' She was still only a learner, she thought giddily, in the glorious subject of what a man and a woman would do together. But, oh, she was learning fast!

The green dress too, alas, would never be the same again. At one point she had caught her foot in the hem, and had torn it a little breaking free. The material was washable, fortunately, and the tear was not too conspicuous; but the dress would never again have that brand-new, sample look about it. She would never be able to show it to a buyer again.

Marcus had been so insistent that she wear it, she thought, suddenly. There had been no need for the ruse, she would have undressed for him willingly enough. But he had said he wanted to see her in it, and she had gone on wearing it until they had finally collapsed in an exhausted, satiated, blissful heap. He had known how it would be. He had known she would never be able to show it afterwards. In fact, the only thing he had not known was that the dress was a reject, that the buyers had turned it down, and that Janis had already decided that it was a failure.

Somehow, what had seemed so spontaneous the night before seemed rather less of a coincidence in the cold light of morning. Marcus had known exactly what he was doing. Exactly what he was looking for, in the studio. He thought he knew what he had found. And he must have thought he knew what it meant, when the green dress ended up as a tangled rag underneath the two of them.

Janis cursed under her breath. She had felt guilty because she had been deceiving him! Why, he must have thought he had it made from the very moment she had taken him up to the studio. One kiss, and she let him trample all over her, take her body *and* wreck her career. Or so he thought.

How lucky it was that she had still hidden the work that really mattered from him. He had no idea, still, of that morning's meeting with the Vane's buyer, when she would hand over three dozen pristine garments in different shapes, colours and sizes.

She pulled into the factory forecourt. It was not quite eight o'clock, and Trenco was deserted. She walked through the empty office, past the silent rows of sewing machines, and into the storeroom. She shifted all the boxes of shirts, packaged together in neat dozens, thirteen and a halves and fourteens and fourteen and a halves. She uncovered the boxes she had hidden behind them, and began to carry them out, a stack at a time, to the yellow Mini. She stacked them in the boot and on the back seat. She put all the boxes of shirts back, so that everything looked exactly as it had when she'd arrived. Then she locked up, got into the car, and set off for her meeting with the Vane's buyer.

CHAPTER EIGHT

'YOU remember the beach barbecue?' Marcus said.

They were sitting in a wine bar, in one of the little roads that led from the promenade to the town centre. It was a basement, low-ceilinged and candle-lit, with a smell of damp corks and garlicky suppers. Marcus had chosen the wine, a deep red, strong and rich-tasting.

Janis grinned. 'Oh, I remember. We never have danced together, you know.'

'I'm a lousy dancer. I was bluffing, that evening; I just wanted an excuse to hold you.'

'It must be . . . nearly a month ago.'

'Seems longer, doesn't it?'

Janis nodded. It was hard to remember that it was barely a week since she had finished the second set of samples, and they had been delivered to the Manchester store. Since then, she had spent every evening with Marcus.

She had even dropped the Monday evening classes, when Marcus insisted that she would do much better to learn about accounting from him. He had tried teaching her that Monday, but after a few moments they had ended up in each other's arms, the balance sheets forgotten. He hadn't given up his squash games, but she had gone over to the sqaush club with him for his league match on Tuesday, watching him play from the balcony, and braving all Roger and Bruce's silly jokes about young love in the bar afterwards. Marcus had baited Roger in return about

Emily, but apparently Emily was not quite besotted enough to watch Roger play squash.

'Not long enough,' she said. Though Marcus, of course, was not conscious of their deadline, as she was. There were only two more weeks left of the month Louise and Bruce had given her. Two weeks to love Marcus, two weeks for the clothes in Vane's Oxford Street store to find buyers. Then somehow she would have to confess, and it would all be over.

'Peter and Cheryl,' Marcus said. Janis frowned, and he went on, 'Bruce and Louise. Andy and Mary. Roger and Emily.'

'Of course, the dinner party Peter and Cheryl arranged! I'm sorry, I'm so dense.'

'I'd forgotten too, but Cheryl phoned to remind me this morning. It's this Friday.'

'Oh. But we hadn't meant to . . . I mean, you and I hadn't . . .'

'You and I weren't a couple a month ago. We are now. The fifth couple: Marcus and Janis.' Marcus gave a satisfied smile.

Janis' heart sank. If they did go, it would be the first time they had faced all their friends together. It was meant to be the first of a whole series of dinners, each couple taking it in turns to entertain the others. It had such an air of permanence about it, going to an evening like that as a couple. Except that she knew that, by the time the next dinner came around, she and Marcus wouldn't even be on speaking terms. And Bruce and Louise knew why, and surely wouldn't be able to resist showing a little curiosity.

'But Emily . . . Wouldn't Emily . . .'

'Mind? Of course not. According to Cheryl, she and Roger are practically engaged already.'

'I did tell you my brother's coming home on Friday

night?'

'You did. He'll still be around on Saturday morning, won't he?'

'Yes. I suppose so.'

'I told Cheryl we'd be there around eight. I'm sure your brother won't mind. After all, it's a long-standing arrangement.'

Janis didn't answer.

'So I'll pick you up at a quarter to eight. It'll take a good quarter of an hour to drive over to Peter and Cheryl's house, it's right on the other side of town. Come to think of it, I should maybe make it seven-thirty, then I can say hello to your brother before we go.'

'You'll like Matthew,' Janis said automatically. Marcus wouldn't, she thought as soon as the words were out. Matthew was so scruffy, so laid-back—as different from Marcus as anyone could be.

'I'm sure I will.' Marcus smiled. 'You'll like Peter and Cheryl, too. I realise you barely know them yet, but they're really looking forward to seeing some more of you.'

It was such a relief to see Matthew coming towards the barrier at the station, disreputable rucksack on his back and duty-free bag in his hand. He fished out a bottle of Scotch and waved it at Janis while he was waiting in the queue to show his ticket. As soon as he was through the barrier, he whirled her round and round in the station forecourt.

'English weather,' he groaned, tossing the rucksack into the back of the Mini. 'It was hot and sunny in Paris yesterday. Look, you have to come over, Jan. You could sleep on my floor.'

'Your floor!' teased Janis.

'Unrepeatable offer! Only open until August. No, honestly, I'll give you my bed and sleep on the floor myself. What more can a man do?'

'It does sound tempting. Very slightly tempting. Maybe next month . . .'

'Honeymoon in Paris?'

'Honeymoon? Matthew, what on earth do you mean?'

Matthew grinned, and took a slug of the Scotch. 'You may never put pen to paper,' he said, 'but Mother writes, you know. Every fortnight, regular as clockwork. She told me all about old Julius Caesar.'

'Who?'

'Well, whatever his name is.'

'Marcus, you idiot.'

'Sounds ideal husband material, from what Mother said.'

Janis glanced across at him, as they were waiting at the traffic lights. It was too tempting to tell him. And it would be too awful, to have him teasing her all weekend.

'Look, Matthew, you have it all wrong. No, shut up a moment and listen. Really, it's a disaster. It's all going to end in a couple of weeks. I guess I might need your floor for a while after that.'

'Janis, love, either it's a disaster and it's finished, or it's fine and it's carrying on. I can't make out this couple-of-weeks business.'

'I'll explain to you, Matthew. Just don't talk about it to Mother, OK?'

'I'll have to say something if I meet him. I *am* going to meet him?'

'Lunch on Sunday. Well, he'll probably be round on Saturday, too.'

'Some disaster! You can tell me about it tonight.'

'I'm going out with him tonight.'

Matthew let out a groan. 'Just give me plenty of warning, Jan. I'll need to save if you expect a wedding present.'

'I don't, I don't!' No hope of that, Janis thought wretchedly to herself.

Peter turned the wire very cautiously. One turn. Two turns. He eased off the little cage, nudged the cork. And pow! the champagne fizzed out of the bottle into a cascade that soaked the tablecloth, Cheryl and everything else within three feet of him.

'Roger and Emily,' he announced, when all their glasses were full.

'Emily and Roger,' Louise corrected loudly. 'You male chauvinist lot!'

'Emily and Roger,' Janis echoed. She couldn't help thinking of honeymoons in Paris. Roger, however, was speculating on much more grandiose lines. Rio de Janeiro. The Taj Mahal. Hong Kong, Bangkok, the Orient Express . . .

'What an end to a dinner,' Mary murmured. 'What a dinner, come to that.'

'We really should have had the champagne at the start, though. Your fault, Roger. You should have told us earlier.'

Roger waved expansively. 'We only decided on the way here tonight. Then it wasn't till we'd had the chicken that I remembered you two are the kind who always have a few bottles of champers in the wine rack.'

'Well, *we're* not,' laughed Andy. 'So, if you plan to pull the same trick next month, Marcus, you'd better give us plenty of warning.'

'We'll try,' Marcus said lightly. Janis could feel his

eyes moving to her, and she turned hurriedly to
Louise, not daring to look at him.

'And what on earth will we do after that?' Cheryl
was moaning. 'Everyone else is married already!'

'Babies, darling,' Louise said brightly, and they all
burst out laughing again.

Janis joined in, though she could still feel a catch in
her throat. It was lucky, in a way, that Emily and
Roger had grabbed all the attention. They had made
such a performance of their snap engagement that
nobody had given her and Marcus much more than a
second glance. But she had had to endure an hour of
her mother's gushing to Matthew about him that
afternoon, and there would be more to come before
Matthew left on Tuesday. Marcus, what was worse,
seemed at times to encourage her mother's specula-
tions. Though at least, she thought to herself, he
would have better taste than to propose to her that
weekend, in the wake of Roger's anouncement. Not
that he could really have been thinking of it, anyway.

She took a big sip of the champagne, and turned to
smile at him, brightly, emptily. He was still looking at
her, a hint of a frown on his face, and his eyes,
meeting hers, provided unexpected reassurance,
melting her fears temporarily and reminding her that,
for two weeks at least, everything was going to be fine.

Matthew and Janis walked slowly along the beach.
Matthew didn't like the empty stretches outside town;
he preferred the main town beaches with their ice-
cream sellers and postcard stands and the bucket-and-
spade brigade. It was a fine Sunday afternoon, and the
day-trippers were out in force.

They wandered under the pier, and Matthew swung
from his arms on the rusted iron struts. The rust came

off on his hands, and he brushed it off, down his denims.

'Cold in the shade, isn't it?'

'Even colder in the water, I should think,' Janis replied.

'You should have come in yesterday, then you'd have found out.'

'Somebody had to stay with Mother,' Janis reminded him.

'We could have taken it in turns. I reckon you were just scared in case Marcus ducked you.'

'Marcus ducked me? It's you who always does the ducking.'

Matthew grinned. 'Yes, but you always used to duck me in return.'

'I'll come in with you before you go back.'

'Now?' Janis hesitated, and Matthew urged her. 'You'll be working tomorrow, and it'll be too cold if we leave it till you finish work. Come on, let's do it now.'

'I haven't got my costume with me, and it's miles back to the house.'

'I'll drive back for it. Go on, say yes.'

Janis laughed. 'Matthew, it's past four o'clock now.'

Matthew made a face. 'Big Sis tells me it's too late. And I know, Big Sis wants a Serious Talk.'

'We do have to talk now, Matthew. This might be the only chance we get without Mother around.'

'You mean, without Marcus around.'

'That, too.'

Matthew glanced at her, and then sat down, suddenly, on the shingle. He waited for Janis to join him, then said, 'I still don't understand what all the drama is about. All this cloak-and-dagger stuff. Don't tell Marcus this, don't tell Mother that. It's not like you, Jan.'

'I know it's not. I hate keeping secrets. That's why I need to tell you, Matthew.'

'OK, here's your Big Chance.'

Janis opened her mouth to tell him off for being so flippant, then saw that, beneath the idiotic gestures, Matthew was looking perfectly serious, even a little worried. 'Right,' she said, and began to explain, as carefully as she could, about Trenco and the new designs.

Matthew rolled on to his stomach and began to build little pyramids of pebbles, but she could sense that he was listening, and she was grateful that he didn't keep interrupting her. When she had finished, he asked a few questions, checking on points she hadn't made clear; and then fell silent.

'You're supposed to say something,' Janis reminded him.

'I'm thinking. *C'est difficile.*'

'Sure is.'

He put a final pebble on his tallest pyramid. 'Do you want me to come back? Throw up the course, and all that?'

'Oh, Matthew, Mother would hate it. And you would too, wouldn't you?'

'Well, it's not really my thing, playing the tycoon. I suppose it was dumb and selfish of me, though; I never really thought of you either, doing the accounts and typing the invoices and all that junk. I was going to be the famous translator and you were going to be the famous designer, weren't you? And now we wake up to the real world.'

'The real world, where Mummy and Daddy have rows about the washing up and worry about money. Where Janet and John go to work in the factory up the road.'

Matthew grinned. 'It's not quite that bad. Actually, I was reckoning on teaching English in Paris.'

'That would suit you, Matthew.'

'Yes, it would,' he agreed. He tried to balance one more pebble on the pile, and then whipped it off again as the rest began to slide beneath it. 'I suppose you'd be mad at me if I told you you were lucky to have Marcus.'

A shiver went through Janis. 'I suppose I would,' she said in a tight, warning voice.

'But I'm going to say it, anyway.' He swept the pile of pebbles away, with an awkward movement of his arm, and then swivelled round and sat up on the shingle. 'Since this is a Truth Session.'

'You haven't been listening, Matthew.'

'Oh, yes, I have. Every word. And I listened to Marcus yesterday, while we were having our arctic swim. I really like him, Jan. He wouldn't do anything to hurt you. He's nuts about you, you must know that.'

'He doesn't understand about the designing.'

'Oh, yes, he does.' Janis began a hot denial, and Matthew silenced her with a glare and a wave of his hand. 'Be fair, Jan. I listened to everything you said. Now it's your turn to listen to me.' He wrapped his hands around his knees, and gazed at her, suddenly intent and serious. 'What on earth do you think Marcus wants, Jan? He doesn't want Trenco. Why should he care about Trenco? It's just a two-bit company, like millions of others. He could pick one up tomorrow if he wanted to play a little power game with writs and takeovers and all that stuff. The only reason Marcus has ever bothered about Trenco is because Trenco is you, and he doesn't want to see you in a mess. What Marcus really wants is for you and he to turn into a nice happy Mummy and Daddy who pay someone else to do the washing up and never have to worry about money. He'll make the dough and you'll do your designing—and, if your clothes sell, fine; if they don't, it won't cost you the roof over your heads.'

Janis bowed her head.

'That's what you want too, isn't it, Jan?' Matthew persisted.

'Oh, Matthew,' she sighed. 'If only it were true. If only it could be like that.'

'Well, make it like that! Go on! Nobody else is going to do it for you.'

'But he's wrong about Trenco. About the shirts and everything.'

'Oh, sure he is.' Matthew said this so airily that Janis looked up, bewildered.

'He's not Superman, Jan,' Matthew said gently. 'Of course he makes mistakes. I can see what you mean about the white shirts and nobody wearing them any more. Guys like me—I don't even own a white shirt. I can see Trenco's got to evolve or die, survival of the fittest and all that. If an idiot like me can see it, Marcus can see it, too. I'll bet that, by now, he knows he misjudged the market when he started. He knows that as soon as the bank are off your backs you'll have to try and diversify a bit. If not sooner.'

'You don't know how hard he's fought me.'

'No, but I can guess how hard you've fought him.' Matthew smiled. 'You're doing what you did when we were kids, Jan. You'd be so damn sure you were right. You'd yell and scream and stamp your foot, absolutely determined not to give an inch. That would make me yell and scream and stamp my foot back at you. Most of the time I was wrong, and half the time I knew it, but you would always get me into a corner where I couldn't afford to admit it. And the harder you stamped your foot, the harder I'd stamp mine back.'

Janis gave him a shaky grin. 'Yes, but how else could I convince you?'

'Convincing me was the easy bit. Getting me to admit I was convinced was tougher. And I bet Marcus is a sight more arrogant and determined and opinionated than I ever was.'

'He is. He is. Oh, Matthew, you might be right. You might be. I'd so like to believe you are. But if you are—what on earth do I do?'

'That's the tough bit. I wish I knew, Jan. I wish I knew. Course, you could drop all this underhand stuff for a start.'

Jan bit her lip. 'He'll be so furious when he finds out.'

'Can't say I blame him. I'd be furious if I was in his shoes.'

'Then *what?*'

'I'm thinking. Give me time, Jan. It's a slow process, my brain working.'

'Fat lot of good you'd be as a split-second translator!'

'I was wrong about that. I was wrong. I admit it. See how easy it is?'

'For some.'

'OK, that wasn't much help. Look, we're getting nowhere here, and the sun's gone in. I'll race you back to the car, and maybe inspiration will strike on the way.'

'Do I get a handicap?'

'A handicap? The lady wants a handicap as well! Oh, go on. I'll let you get back to the pier before I start.'

Janis scrambled to her feet, took a deep breath, and began to run, weaving through the startled day-trippers with their deckchairs and their windbreaks and their ice-creams.

Matthew caught her on the promenade. He ran fifty yards ahead of her, and then stopped and turned, waving his arms in the air to slow her down.

'We're not there yet,' Janis panted.

'I know. Hey, that was a mean trick of yours, making for the first set of steps.'

'It's hard work running on the shingle.'

'True.' Matthew leaned against the iron railing that protected the drop down to the beach below. 'To be honest, sis, I forgot where on earth we'd parked the car.'

'Matthew!'

'And,' he added, suddenly triumphant, 'inspiration struck.'

Janis joined him by the railings. 'Go on, then.'

'You resign from Trenco.'

'I *what?* Matthew, you're not serious.'

'Absolutely serious. No, think about it, Jan. You

have to tell Marcus what you've done. You have to show him you know it was rotten of you. You have to show him you trust him now, even if you do think he was wrong. So why not resign? Let him have the company, and then he'll be in a position to do his generous act. Can't you see, there's nothing to lose? Even if I'm wrong, and it's the one thing he wanted from the start, you have to admit he'd run the company very well. Mother wouldn't lose out, I'm sure. And, if he won't take your new designs on board, you can set up your own little company to sell them yourself.'

Janis frowned. 'There has to be a catch.'

'Probably dozens. But you'll think about it?'

The frown knitted her face for a moment longer, and then she relaxed, and turned to Matthew. 'OK. I'll think about it.'

Matthew drove the Mini back to White Gates, while Janis thought. It was funny. She'd fought so hard to retain control of Trenco, yet the sudden suggestion that she should give it all up to Marcus was oddly appealing to her. In a sense, Marcus had been right all along. She had never wanted to be a tycoon. She had always wanted to be a designer, not to run a shirt factory, and there was something exhilarating about the thought of letting somebody else take over the invoices and the order chasing, permanently.

It couldn't mean that, though. Orders and invoices were real life, they were the Janet-and-John things that couldn't be set aside. Trenco couldn't yet afford to hire someone else to do them, while Janis worked full time as a designer. The mucky jobs would always be hers, for as long as she and Matthew and her mother needed to earn a living from the struggling company. And they did. They couldn't sell Trenco, not in its present position: it still wouldn't make enough to repay the bank loan. They couldn't live on what Janis earned as a free-lance designer.

No, she couldn't abandon the company, even if she did resign her position on the Board. It would have to mean working for Trenco still, but for Marcus's Trenco, not her own. It would mean accepting his policies from then onwards, however much she disagreed with them.

There was also the problem of her mother and Mr Jenkins. It wouldn't do to tell either of them precisely what had been happening over the past few months. It wouldn't be fair to risk exposing what Marcus had done, before Trenco was safely in the black. Resigning might seem to be a condemnation of his actions, instead of the vote of confidence that she intended it to be.

'I could join the board in your place,' Matthew offered.

Janis thought. No, that would solve nothing.

'I could join the board in Mother's place, then.'

'Matthew! You don't understand. It means such a lot to Mother, being on the board. I know she does next to nothing, but it's ever so important to her.'

'So are you.'

'But it wouldn't help, Matthew.'

'How about this, then? You don't resign. You stay on the board, in nominal charge of the whole show. But you come clean to Marcus, and then you plead exhaustion and come back with me to Paris. Leave it all for a month or so, sign a book of blank cheques or whatever it takes, and let Marcus do exactly what he likes with the company. Including the orders for your designs. That ought to convince him.'

Janis was silent. Matthew turned into Roselea Crescent, and stopped the mini in the drive of White Gates.

'I've still got two weeks,' she said slowly.

'You coward. You unspeakable coward, Janis Trench! You come back with me on Tuesday, or not at all. Offer closes Tuesday morning.'

'You said it was open till August!'

'I've changed my mind.'

'I'd have to go into Trenco on Tuesday. Marcus will be there on Monday, I wouldn't be able to fix anything then.'

'That's OK. We wouldn't have to leave till three.'

'I haven't any money. No credit. Nothing at all.'

'Trenco must owe you some holiday pay. You haven't taken any time off at all since Dad died, have you? Write yourself a fat cheque on Tuesday morning. You can do that, surely.'

'Mother will be horrified.'

'I'll deal with Mother.'

'What if Marcus follows me to Paris?'

'I told you that was what you needed. A honeymoon in Paris. See?'

'You seem to have all the answers,' Janis said weakly.

'Amazing, isn't it?' Matthew agreed. 'I never knew I had it in me.'

Matthew came with Janis to the factory on Monday morning. He persuaded Marcus to show him the computer system, and he raved over all the clever touches that Marcus had put into it. Janis was uneasily conscious that she had always been too jealous and suspicious herself to show how much she appreciated his work.

They went to lunch at an Indian restaurant on the main road, taking Anthea along as well. The two men argued about trade and politics and shirt styles and the best places to swim on the coast, and Janis listened and watched them, still astonished to find how well they got on. They looked so different, Marcus the smart accountant and Matthew the scruffy student, but they shared many ideas and attitudes, and seemed to be instinctively in sympathy with each other.

Matthew turned the conversation to Paris and the university, and was astonished to learn that Marcus had never been there.

'It's one of those places I've always just missed,' Marcus explained. 'I've been to Brittany and to the South of France, and to most other European countries, but I never felt the inclination to visit Paris alone. I've always been waiting for the right person to come with me.'

He smiled across the table at Janis. 'You haven't been there either, have you, darling? We'll discover Paris together. It would be nice to go this summer, before Matthew leaves. You could find us somewhere to stay, couldn't you, Matthew?'

'A honeymoon in Paris,' Matthew couldn't resist saying. 'A little hotel on the Left Bank, or maybe in Montmartre. Lumpy feather beds and croissants for breakfast.'

Janis was scarlet. 'Not so fast, Matthew,' she murmured.

'We went there for our honeymoon,' Anthea said cheerfully. 'A ten-day package holiday. Dennis spent the whole time complaining about the price of coffee in the cafés. We went to the Eiffel Tower and when he saw how much it cost, he wouldn't go up to the top. And ooh, my feet ached by the time we got home!'

'You obviously married the wrong man, Anthea,' Matthew laughed.

'That I did! I knew it in no time, but it took me another five years to get away from him. Still, it's never too late to try again. I met a lovely plumber at a disco on Saturday night.' She turned to Janis. 'He said he knew of some building jobs going, one that might suit Stella's husband. It would be nice to see everybody as happy as you two, wouldn't it?'

'Wonderful,' agreed Janis, wishing that the floor would open and swallow her up.

She went round to Louise's bungalow that evening, while Marcus was playing squash with Bruce, and explained to Louise what she was planning. She rushed back to White Gates and packed her suitcase, leaving Matthew to invent a story for their mother that would explain the rush departure. She reached the squash club in time to join Marcus at the bar and commiserate with Bruce on losing. And she allowed herself a stiff drink before setting off with him back to his flat.

'I like Matthew so much,' Marcus said, as they went up in the lift from the car park. 'I really did enjoy seeing your family over the weekend. I couldn't wait, though, to get you alone for a while.'

Janis smiled, remembering the snatched kisses in

his car, on the beach, in her studio. There had never been more than a couple of minutes before her mother or Matthew had called out to see where they were, when they were coming. Long enough to whet their appetite, not nearly long enough to satisfy it. Her appetite for Marcus would never be satisfied, except temporarily. But that evening, she knew, might be the last they ever spent together.

Even if Matthew was right—and though she longed to believe him, she still had lingering doubts—it would be the last time she saw Marcus for a month. However he reacted to her confession, it was hardly likely that he would be able to drop all his work and follow her to Paris. She couldn't destroy the evening, she thought now, by making her confession to him then. She needed just this little bit more of him. One perfect memory, to carry with her to Paris.

Marcus dumped his squash kit by the door, and followed her into his living-room. It was still early, and beyond the big windows she would see the view of the sea that he had insisted he would always have, wherever he lived or worked. She crossed the room and stood, drinking it in. A moment later he joined her, and slipped an arm round her waist.

'You haven't met my brothers yet. Or my parents. I want to take you up to York with me to see them. Perhaps next weekend, if that's all right with your mother. We could take off the Monday, and perhaps Tuesday too, so we don't need to rush. Stop on the way, maybe. Anthea knows the system now, she can run Trenco for us.'

'I'd have to talk to Mother.'

'It's not Paris, I know, but we'll get to Paris before

too long. Later this year, I hope.'

Janis moved, burying her head in his shoulder. He smelled of soap and shampoo, from the showers at the squash club. She felt Marcus's arms tighten round her, and his cheek rub against her hair. And wondered how on earth she would bear it, if Matthew turned out to be wrong, after all.

CHAPTER NINE

A STICK of French bread under one arm, and a bag full of groceries in the other hand, Janis tramped up the flights of steps towards Matthew's tiny apartment. Everyone in Paris, it seemed, lived up umpteen flights of stairs. Nowhere were there lifts, and all the stairs were filthy, with that lingering smell of garlic and cabbage and cat that was even more Parisian that Gauloises.

The only thing that varied was the kind of apartment to be found behind the uniformly blank front doors. Some of those she had been in were beautifully decorated, spotless and charming. Matthew's, alas, was a typical student dump, scruffy and noisy and overcrowded. It had been unspeakably dirty when she'd arrived, and Matthew still groaned loudly whenever she attempted to empty the sink of washing up or run a broom across the kitchen floor. It ruined his Bohemian image, he complained, when she stopped him living in picturesque squalor.

'Picturesque! You call this picturesque?' Janis had cried, waving a despairing arm at the festering piles of dirty washing.

'Why not? Still life with purple underpants. Hang on, hang on, I said *still* life!' Matthew protested as his sister hurled the offending garments at him, one by one.

It was fun, in a way. The sights of Paris were all smaller and grubbier and older, somehow, than Janis had expected, and the cafés on the Champs-Elysées, she had discovered, fully justified all Anthea's Dennis's complaints. But the food was wonderful everywhere, the sun was shining, Matthew's friends were friendly, the student clubs and bars were full of life, and the Mona Lisa was still the Mona Lisa, even when you had to peer at her from the back of a crowd of tourists ten deep. In fact, the only thing that was missing was Marcus.

Oh, how she missed Marcus! If only he had been there to share everything with her, she knew, Paris would have taken on that indefinable glamour that, as it was, it just did not have for her. Even the disasters would have been wonderful if Marcus had been there to share them. The real wonders would have been ten times more wonderful. But he wasn't there, and she couldn't help counting the days until she was back in Smithbury, and she saw him again.

A phone call would have helped, but Matthew had made her promise on the boat that she wouldn't phone Marcus, her mother or Trenco at all, not even once. Marcus, though he could easily have got her number from her mother, had very definitely not phoned her.

She wished, now, that she had been less of a coward, and had told him face to face about the Vane's buyer and the sample contracts. She wished even more that the whole wretched affair had never happened. But she couldn't change it now. She couldn't change a word of the letter she had left, sealed, on Marcus's desk at Trenco, with the carbon copies of the two orders, the cheque from Vane's that she hadn't dared pay into the company account, and the stubs of the cheques that she'd written out on Tuesday morning to repay Louise and herself.

She deserved to have faced his explosion when he learned what she had done. She deserved to have been shouted at. She deserved to have had Marcus storming out of the office and slamming the door behind him. But if she had been there, in Smithbury, she could have run after him, pleaded, cried, grovelled apologies until he knew that he meant infinitely more to her than Trenco ever would. As it was, the explosion would surely have happened just the same, but without her as the vital witness. He might have stormed out just the same, but nobody would have come running after him. He might even have ripped her carefully composed letter to shreds, before he got beyond the confessions and into the capitulations. Anything, anything might have happened to him. The anguish of it was that she didn't know which of her imaginings were true.

I'm going back tomorrow. She had said that to Matthew almost every day since she had arrived. Matthew had laughed and teased and told her she didn't trust Marcus enough, and that she must, must, *must* give him the month they had agreed on.

Three weeks of it were up. One week to go, and then Matthew would pour a last glass of wine, accompany her to the Gare du Nord, and hold out his hand for her unused metro tickets. One week, and she would be on the boat back to England. One week, and she would be retrieving her car from the long-stay car park at Dover and driving back to Smithbury. One week, and she would be home again.

One week. She dumped the *baguette* in the string bag that hung from the side of the cupboard on the kitchen wall. One week. She put the bottle of *Vin Rouge du Table* on the counter by the sink. One week. She opened the fridge and stowed away the *saucisson* and the pâté. One week. She hunted through the cupboard for a bowl that would hold the kilo of cherries when she'd washed them. One week. She sat down at the kitchen table, and began to chop up carrots and onions and potatoes, to make an enormous pan full of soup to feed Matthew and his vast and fluctuating horde of friends and flatmates.

Marcus hadn't been to White Gates. He hadn't phoned, he hadn't called round, he hadn't spoken to her mother. Janis found this out in the first ten minutes after she arrived back home. Her mother spent the next hour asking her what exactly had happened, and peering over her shoulder as if she somehow expected Marcus to appear. What on earth had Matthew told her? Janis wondered, tired and exasperated. Nothing, probably. She didn't dare to ask.

She left her things half unpacked, and as soon as she had finished the obligatory welcoming cup of tea she set off for the factory. That was where she had left her message to him. She wanted to check there first.

It was eight-thirty in the evening, and raining lightly. The industrial estate had that grimy, half-sized, half-familiar look that places seen every day take on after a few weeks' absence. The main door to Trenco was locked. There were no cars parked outside, no lights on.

Janis unlocked the door and let herself in. She walked down the corridor and went into the office.

It was all changed round. Anthea's desk was in the corner, and her own desk had been moved to where it had been before Marcus had come. The computer was perched on the end of it. The new filing cabinets were there, the familiar plants and calendars and posters. Marcus's desk was just by the door. It was empty, and it looked as if it was waiting for the removers.

Woodenly, Janis walked over to her desk.

It was all spread out across the middle, where she would see it as she sat down. A print-out of the latest balance sheet, showing that they were now marginally, very marginally, in the black. A carbon copy of an order from Vane's for a thousand tops in assorted colours and sizes, with tight delivery dates and terms so good that she knew Marcus must have wrung the Vane's buyer to within an inch of her life. Copies of half a dozen other orders that had come in while she was away. And, at the end of the row, a single sheet of paper with Anson and Williams' blue letterhead.

There was only one paragraph. It stated, baldly and formally, that Marcus Anson was resigning as a director of Trenco. It was dated that day. It was signed 'M H Anson' in his familiar, sloping scrawl. There was a note on the bottom to show that a carbon copy had already gone to Mr Jenkins at the bank.

He hadn't bothered to seal it in an envelope. He had just left it, where he knew she would see it as soon as she sat down. There was nothing else. No note for her at all, no letter, no kind of message.

Janis sat there for a long time. She hadn't switched

the lights on, and it grew dark in the office. After a while, she couldn't see the writing on the papers at all, except for that black, accusing signature. She got up then, went out of the office, locked up behind her, and went to sit in her car.

It was a rejection, she knew that, but she drove into town anyway, and rang the doorbell of his flat for ten minutes before she admitted to herself that he wasn't going to answer it. She drove past Anson and Williams too, but the lights were all out, and she knew he wasn't there.

It was ten-thirty by then, and she drove home, went up to her room, and lay down, fully clothed, on her bed. She lay there for a long time, staring blank-eyed at the ceiling. The next thing she knew, her mother was there with a morning cup of tea, and she was getting up with an aching head and a dry feeling in her mouth.

'I thought you must have talked about it.' Anthea was embarrassed, apologetic and incurably curious. 'It was all so matter of fact. He came in just the same while you were away, a bit quiet really, but I thought that was just because you weren't around, and worked, and showed me a bit more of how to run the system. Then yesterday he got me to type out the letter and post a copy to Mr Jenkins, and he moved all the stuff out of his desk drawers, and I helped him move his desk over here.' Anthea looked down. She was sitting on the bare top of Marcus's desk. 'Then we went for a drink in the pub, Scotch for him and a Babycham for me, and he said thanks for everything I'd done, and I said how pleased you'd be about the Vane's order, and then he went.'

'He didn't say anything else?'

'No. Well, I didn't ask. You know what Marcus is like when he doesn't want to be asked about something. I could see you'd had a row, the way he read the letter you left, and then went out without saying anything, and came back, oh, hours later—it must have been nearly lunch-time. You might have warned me about it.'

'I'm sorry, Anthea. I'm sorry. Look, just leave me alone this morning. Take the morning off. Go and do some shopping.'

'You're sure?' Anthea could see she wasn't going to get a reply. She grabbed her bag and slipped out of the office.

When she had gone, Janis phoned Anson and Williams. Mr Anson was away for the week, his secretary told her. Did she want to speak to Mr Williams instead? Janis said no. The secretary said she would tell Mr Anson Janis had called.

She phoned his flat, and listened to the sound of the phoning ringing and ringing in the distance. Then she asked Stella to mind the office, and drove into Smithbury. She rang his doorbell. No reply. She went down into the underground garage and saw that the dark blue Jaguar was missing.

When she got back to the office, Stella told her Mr Jenkins had phoned. Mechanically, she rang the bank.

'Miss Trench, this really is most irregular.' Mr Jenkins was direct and shirty and not at all his bumbling, familiar self. Janis let him grumble on about lack of warning, and overdue board meetings, and feeling kept in the dark about the financial position.

When he stopped for breath, she promised him she would arrange a board meeting for the following week.

'I want Mr Anson replaced,' Mr Jenkins repeated, metronomically. 'I want him replaced immediately. I shall have to telephone him and find out what's behind all this.'

Janis dug her fingernails into her palm. 'He's away at the moment, Mr Jenkins,' she said.

'I must have an explanation. This is an extremely disturbing.'

Janis dug her fingernails in deeper, and invited Mr Jenkins to come over to Trenco that afternoon. She would show him the figures and convince him, at least, that Trenco was not about to go bankrupt. Mr Jenkins grumbled and fudged and finally told her he was much too busy, and he would send the assistant manager over instead.

Janis switched on the computer. She prayed, while it was going through its switch-on memory check, that Marcus would have programmed in some kind of message to her. She hunted through the directories of programs and worked all through the accounting screens, but there was nothing. All the passwords and different access levels had gone. All the figures were up to date. He had entered the sample contracts, and had set up graphs which showed her how much money they had lost. It was more than she had expected. She could see, looking at his costings, how many factors she had overlooked. She erased these and the graphs; they were only meant for her. He had entered the Vane's contract, and revised all his profit forecasts to show how it would affect Trenco. The forecasts were good. She knew the assistant bank manager would be reassured.

It was oddly comforting to think that Marcus hadn't paved the ground with Mr Jenkins. If he had simply been trying to salvage his pride, Janis thought, he would have spent the month working up his excuses and explanations, producing a foolproof cover story, even setting up a few traps to embarrass her in revenge. He had done none of that, as far as she could see. He had just finished getting Trenco into order, and pulled out to lick his wounds.

He had surely told Peter Williams something, though. She had to know what, before she was trapped into lying to Mr Jenkins, or the assistant bank manager, or even her mother. She took a deep breath, and phoned Anson and Williams again.

'Janis.' Peter Williams sounded breezy and reassuring. 'I thought you'd phone this morning. I'm with a client now, but I've an hour free over lunch, from one to two. Could you come over here?'

Underneath the charm, it sounded like an order. Janis agreed to go over. It was twelve already. She spent an hour flicking through the mountain of post that had built up for her, and preparing for the assistant bank manager's visit.

Peter Williams didn't have a sea view. Otherwise, his office was much like Marcus's. His secretary had fixed coffee and a tray of sandwiches. Janis looked at them blankly. Politely pressed, she picked one up. Eating didn't occur to her.

Peter knew that she and Marcus were through. Marcus had evidently made that very clear. All Peter knew, as far as Janis could gather from his repeated commiserations, was that the two of them had split up, and that, in the circumstances, Marcus wanted to get out of Trenco.

'Where is he?' Janis asked.

'He's taken a week off. He's had a heavy year, Janis, and he needed a break.'

'Where?'

'If you've an urgent problem, I'll do what I can to sort it out for you. I'm a little tied up this week, but we've several people who are familiar with the sort of system Marcus set up for you, and I can easily send one of them over.'

'Where, Peter? Where?'

'Look, Janis, why don't you come round and talk to Cheryl this evening? She's much better at this kind of thing than I am.'

'Peter, where is he?'

'Janis, please calm down. Honestly, I don't know where he is. He said he'd phone in this afternoon. Let him have this week. If you need to talk things over, it can wait till next week.'

Next week seemed an eternity away. A month without Marcus, and then a week without Marcus, and then . . . Janis couldn't make herself believe that she could survive longer than that without Marcus.

'We did talk over the directorship,' Peter was saying, briskly, to hide his embarrassment. 'These things often happen in family firms, directors falling out with each other and resigning, but it's always difficult. Of course, a different firm of accountants could fulfil the same function, but I'd like Anson and Williams to keep the business, and I wouldn't want

Jack Jenkins to get the wrong impression. I thought it might be best, in the circumstances, if I suggested to him that I replace Marcus on the board, if that would be acceptable to you and your mother. The system is all in place now, so it would just be a matter of meeting once a month or so, checking over the figures, working up some forecasts and so on. There would be no reason at all for you to see Marcus, so I hope you wouldn't find it too upsetting. Cheryl liked you so much, and I do hope we'll both stay in personal contact with you.'

Keeping the business. Earning the fees. Pacifying Mr Jenkins at the bank. It all sounded so cold and businesslike. It had all been so different, with Marcus. Janis bit her lip.

'If you feel even that would be too painful at the moment, I'd be happy to suggest another firm . . .'

Life was too painful right then in any case. Meeting Peter Williams once a month was hardly going to make it any worse. And she didn't want Marcus to think she was being vindictive, refusing Peter's offer. She didn't want Marcus to think she didn't love him, because he wouldn't forgive her. She wanted every excuse she could find to hear about him, know what he was doing, how he was, see him . . .

'Thanks, Peter.'

'I really am sorry Marcus didn't handle this better. He only told me yesterday. Otherwise we could have talked it over with Jenkins before he sent in his resignation, and arranged a much smoother transition. But I'll give Jack a ring this afternoon, and it should all be sorted out in no time.'

'You'll tell me how it goes.'

'Naturally. Then there will be the formalities to arrange, the letter of appointment, the records at Companies House to amend, Trenco's letterhead to change . . .'

'I know just what to do.'

'Fine, fine. And, if you need any advice in the meantime, you know where to turn.'

Telling her mother was harder, because Elizabeth Trench still had no idea what had happened. Janis settled for telling her Peter's version, that she and Marcus had split up and that he had resigned, without any more explanation. Elizabeth's accusations followed her around the house. She should never have gone to Paris, he must have thought she wanted to finish with him; she should have phoned him; she should have written; how could she do it? Marcus was so wonderful, she'd never find another man like him . . . It was an immense relief when the telephone rang.

It was Louise. 'Cheryl told me,' she said bluntly. 'And you're coming over. Now.'

'I won't be very good company, Louise.'

'But I will. I'll see you in ten minutes.'

It took fifteen to drive over through the early evening traffic. By then, Louise had banished Bruce to the squash club, put on a soothing Mozart record, located two glasses and opened a bottle of wine.

'I'm getting a bit low on cooking brandy,' she explained, 'and I thought we needed a change. I know you've been talking about it all day, but Cheryl didn't seem to know anything about this business with the secret contracts, so you must have been sticking to a cover story. Now, what really happened? Have you seen Marcus? What did he say?'

'Nothing. No. Nothing.'

'Nothing happened, you haven't seen him, and he didn't say anything?'

'Yes.'

'It always sounds better,' Louise said, 'when you have to answer "yes".'

Janis choked a sort of a laugh, and then found herself dissolving into floods of tears.

'You're diluting the wine. Here, have one of Bruce's hankies.'

Janis sobbed until the record stopped, and then wiped her face and blew her nose loudly into Bruce's enormous handkerchief.

'Now that's over with, perhaps we can talk.'

'Louise, what am I going to do?'

'It really was a dumb idea, you know, going to Paris. Matthew can be idiotic sometimes. So can you, come to that.'

'It seemed to make sense when Matthew suggested it. Louise, have you seen him? Has he been around?'

'Not round here, he hasn't. Bruce and Andy have seen him at the squash club, but they didn't exactly talk. You know what men are like. Bruce said, "I hear Janis is away," and Marcus said, "Yes, she is," and then they argued about the test-match scores or something.'

'He must have talked to somebody.'

'I doubt it. Men like Marcus just don't. Andy phoned him when he was fixing the dinner—you know, we had the dinner at Andy and Mary's last Friday—and Marcus said you were away and he wasn't coming. We all talked about the two of you over dinner, but nobody even realised you'd split up.'

'Nor did I,' Janis said ruefully.

'But you have?'

Janis nodded. 'He told Peter we had. And the letter he left—well, it didn't leave much room for hope.'

'Angry accusations?'

'Oh, no. Very formal. "I herewith tender my resignation" and all that.'

'Tear it up,' Louise suggested.

'I can't. He sent a copy to Mr Jenkins at the bank.'

Louise thought. 'Maybe that isn't a bad thing, you know, Janis. The two of you were arguing so hard about the business. Somebody had to throw in the towel, and you always knew it couldn't be you. So I guess Marcus decided it would have to be him.'

'I wouldn't mind that so much, if he hadn't thrown me over as well.'

'Oh, Janis! You don't still think he was after the bloody company all along?'

Janis gulped, and shook her head. 'No, I don't think that. Not any more. He was fighting me, but I was fighting him, too. Matthew was right, we had to break the deadlock. But then I had to tell him I'd been cheating, taking on the sample contracts behind his back, and—he won't forgive me for that, Louise.'

'Because you were right?'

'I wasn't right. Not absolutely. Those sample contracts cost us an absolute fortune. I didn't even pay myself for all the work in the evenings, the designing and the making up and the delivery, but I had to pay Stella time and a half, and there was no margin in them, and—Louise, it was an awful risk. If the follow-up order hadn't come through, it would have finished us. Broken the company entirely. He'd left all the figures for me so I could see that, all the graphs up on the computer system. I should have checked out the costing more carefully, weighed up the risks, but I was so keen to get the contracts and prove Marcus wrong that I didn't do it. I told myself it would be all right, and it was, but it so easily could not have been. I should have trusted him, Louise, and I didn't, and he won't forgive me for that.'

Louise drank some more wine. 'Did I ever tell you,' she said quietly, 'about my night with Andy?'

'Andy? Louise, what on earth do you mean?'

'That's not really a fair question. I didn't tell you. I know I didn't tell you, because I didn't tell anyone. But Bruce found out all the same.'

'Louise! You slept with Andy, and . . .'

'And Bruce found out. It was while we were engaged. Oh, it was all stupid, there was never anything deep between us. We'd been seeing a lot of each other, Mary and Andy and Bruce and I. You know, that was back in the days when Bruce and Andy shared a flat. Andy and I had this flirtation going, you know, jokes and kisses, and we found ourselves on our own in the flat one night, and the whole thing just got out of hand. Then Bruce came back unexpectedly, and found us together.'

'Oh, my God!'

'That's mild, compared to what Bruce said. He bashed Andy, and threw a few things around, and swore at us, and stormed out, slamming the door behind him. By the time I'd made myself decent enough to go after him, he'd disappeared. You know

Bruce, he's so easygoing normally. He never usually loses his temper. It finished us for nearly a month.'

'I had no idea.'

'I know,' Louise said. 'I didn't tell anyone, because I was so determined to make it up with him. I gave it a week, and then I went round and cried and pleaded and grovelled and told him I couldn't bear it and I loved him so much. Awful, it was. I blush to think of it now, with me usually so liberated and laid-back. But it was true, I couldn't bear to lose him. And I reckoned, underneath all the hurt, he couldn't bear to lose me either.'

'Of course he couldn't.'

'Exactly. I know it was unspeakable of me, and it was asking a lot of him, but he loved me, and I knew it, and you do ask a lot of people you love. You have to sometimes. Bruce has done some pretty unspeakable things too, you know. It wouldn't be fair to tell you about them, but they happened. When I found out about them I was hurt, and angry, and upset, and then when I'd had a chance to calm down I thought to myself, heavens, I don't want to lose Bruce over this. It's the last thing I want. So when he did his apologetic act I let myself be won back again. By now, they're all as good as forgotten, and Bruce and Andy are as good friends as ever, and we both know that it's stupid and rotten to hurt each other, but that if stupid things do happen, neither of us is going to let them break our marriage without a fight.'

'You're so lucky, Louise.'

'There are times,' Louise said grimly, 'when I didn't feel it. You're lucky too, you know. You've found your man. And, if you've any sense at all, you won't let him go without giving it everything you've got. He's too good to lose, Janis. Too right for you.'

'Now,' Janis groaned, 'you sound like my mother again!'

Somehow, the week went past. Though Marcus had run Trenco tightly while Janis was away in Paris, there were still a host of jobs waiting for her now she was back. There was the big new contract to organise, and there were more buyers to see, and shirts to deliver, and she knew she would have to start work very soon on a spring collection. Stella's husband had got a job with Anthea's plumber friend, but Stella was still willing to do some overtime, and so were one or two of the other women. Anthea was keen to take over the accounting system now that she had got the hang of it, and Janis began to think of promoting her and hiring another girl to act as a secretary. Trenco's new shape was beginning to emerge, and the bank were pacified, enthusiastic even, with little hints that, in a month or two, they might be happy to talk about expansion finance.

Expansion? No, Janis didn't want to expand. She didn't want to keep on running Trenco at all. She had reconciled herself so easily to the prospect of handing over to Marcus, and she couldn't regain her enthusiasm for administering the company. She found it hard even to enthuse over the prospect of the spring designs, though she told herself firmly that that was just a temporary low, and she would recover her spirits soon. When Marcus was back.

Peter had been vague about exactly when Marcus was expected back. Janis wrote Marcus a letter, carefully low-key, telling him that she missed him and wanted to see him and talk things over. She posted it by hand under the door of his flat, so that he'd know she had called round to look for him.

He had resigned on a Wednesday. She delivered the letter on Tuesday evening, and he wasn't back then. She waited till Wednesday evening, and then she phoned him.

He answered almost immediately. 'Darling——' Janis began, as a tide of relief swept through her. She was half-way through her second sentence before she realised that Marcus had put the phone down.

She drove round to his flat. She knew, as soon as she reached the door, that he wasn't there. She rang the doorbell for several minutes anyway. Then she sat down on the floor of the corridor outside his front door, and waited.

It was eleven-thirty before he came back. Janis had been dozing off, though it was dreadfully uncomfortable on the corridor floor. The whine of the lift woke her, and she waited apprehensively, as it ground to a halt, the lift doors opened, and Marcus stepped out.

Janis stumbled to her feet. He looked exactly the same. Almost exactly. A little tired, a little dishevelled. He wasn't expecting her to be there, and she watched as his weary expression changed, and a flash of emotion charged his face, only to be suppressed so quickly and so completely that she wondered if she had imagined it simply because she longed so much for him to be glad to see her.

He wasn't glad any more. He strode down the corridor and stopped a pace away from her.

'Get out,' he said.

'Marcus, we have to talk.'

'No.'

'Darling, I have to explain to you——'

'You've already explained,' Marcus said icily. 'Now get out.'

'Please, Marcus.' Janis reached out her hand. He saw it coming, and moved away from her. His keys were in his hand. He circled round to his door, and unlocked it.

Janis moved forward when the door was open.

'No,' Marcus repeated, stepping through it. He made to shut the door, realised her foot and hand were in the way, opened it again, took her by the shoulders and moved her back a couple of paces, and then shut the door. Firmly, right in her face.

Janis burst into tears. She was still crying when the door of the adjoining flat opened and Marcus's neighbour, in his dressing-gown, asked her if she was feeling all right, and whether she might go and do her howling a little further away from his bedroom. That was when she admitted defeat and went home.

CHAPTER TEN

THE trouble with Louise's plan, Janis thought ruefully, was that it did assume a tiny bit of co-operation
from one's partner. You couldn't really weep and
grovel and plead without an audience. Marcus, unfortunately, had no intention whatsoever of acting as her
audience.

She was perfectly willing to do everything she could
to get him back. There was no use doing anything,
though, unless Marcus had just a hint of an intention,
however deeply buried, of coming back to her. He
didn't. He had made that painfully, agonisingly,
abundantly clear to her.

She had managed to see him twice more in the week
after he'd returned. Both times he had presented her
with a blank, impenetrable wall of indifference. He
was warned, now, and there was no way she was going
to catch him off guard again, even for a split second.
Both times he had told her, coldly and firmly, that
there was nothing for them to talk about, that if she
had any problems at Trenco she should talk to Peter,
and that he would be grateful if she kept out of his
way in future.

It was desperately hurtful. It would have been
marginally more bearable if Janis had kept on
believing that Marcus had always wanted Trenco
rather than her; but Matthew and Louise, well

meaning and trying to help, had convinced her that
Marcus really loved her. She knew she really loved
him. But, while her love was the kind that would, she
was sure, have managed to overcome the kind of hurt
that she had inflicted, his very obviously was not.

That was not only hard to bear, it was hard to
understand. All right, she had been wrong. She had
deceived him, she had risked the company's future.
But she had done it for very understandable reasons,
reasons that made sense to Matthew and Louise and
Bruce and everybody else who knew what had
happened, even if they didn't all agree with her. They
were reasons that Marcus had known all about. He
might have been furious, he might have been disappointed, but surely he hadn't been all that
surprised?

Marcus had always known what she wanted to do.
He had known how strongly she disagreed with his
policies for the company. The only thing he hadn't
known was that she was actually working behind his
back. And what did that prove? Simply that the
distrust she had never pretended to hide from him was
very real; that the concern for Trenco she had always
admitted to had caused her to act when she doubted
his judgement.

He hadn't even worked to overcome her distrust,
Janis recalled to herself. He hadn't encouraged her
even to sound out buyers, when that would have cost
them nothing. He had seen some of her work, he
knew she had prepared some designs, and he had
never suggested any way in which she might have
shown them without risking Trenco's future on their
reception. He had destroyed the green dress. Well,

not absolutely destroyed it, since it was washed and mended now and sitting in the back of her wardrobe, but done his best to destroy it.

All this might have made Janis angry but, though she worked a couple of times at developing a good head of steam to let off, she found she couldn't be angry with Marcus. She loved him too much for that. She only wished he had loved her enough in return.

She needed to forget him, she knew, but she couldn't bring herself to try and forget him yet. When Cheryl rang to invite her over to supper, she accepted the invitation enthusiastically, eager to hear anything Cheryl and Peter could tell her about Marcus.

This was a misconception, she realised as soon as she arrived at their house. Peter and Cheryl's idea of a quiet supper consisted of eight people eating four courses, complete with quantities of wine. There was not the remotest possibility of probing them for information about Marcus in front of four total strangers and the elderly bachelor accountant who, Cheryl had politely tried to convey to Janis, had been invited purely to make the numbers up and definitely not as a date for her.

Whenever anyone mentioned Marcus, however casually, Peter or Cheryl adroitly steered the conversation in a different direction. They changed the subject whenever anyone spoke of marriages and engagements and the love-life of mutual acquaintances. Only over the cheese did they relax a little. Evidently, Janis thought, they had decided by then that she was over the weepy stage, and could be trusted not to break down and embarrass everyone.

Janis was trying to tell the elderly accountant about

Trenco—not easy, when she didn't want to mention Marcus herself, and when it wouldn't have done to explain about their financial disasters. She settled for trying to describe her designs, and was surprised to have Cheryl join in enthusiastically. For someone Janis had never directly discussed her work with, Cheryl seemed to know a great deal about the sort of clothes she designed, the colours she preferred, the plans she had.

'Did Louise tell you about my clothes?' Janis asked.

Cheryl flushed. 'No,' she said, trapped. 'Marcus did. Oh, ages ago. He used to talk about it quite a lot.'

'There was never that much to talk about,' Janis said bitterly.

'Oh, Janis, there was! He told us how hard you were working in the evenings, on your new range. Those bright-coloured tops you'd designed. Don't you remember, Peter, we wanted to ask Janis round that night the Jacksons came? Marcus said you were working nearly every evening then, and asked us to leave it for a while.'

'Can't say I do, darling,' Peter said quickly. 'Giles, did I tell you about that time Cheryl and I went to Venice, and . . .'

Those coloured tops. The brightly coloured tops she had been working so hard on in the evenings. There had been no brightly coloured tops on view in her studio, the night Marcus had come for the factory key. He had seen the sketches for the shirtwaisters then, and the loose jacket she had been so pleased with. She had made sure the same shirtwaisters were hanging in the studio the night she had taken him up there. He had flicked through her portfolio that night, but there had been no designs for coloured tops. Because it was the coloured tops that the Vane's buyer had liked and ordered, and all the sketches and samples for the coloured tops were hidden in the factory.

The factory, where she had worked so hard in the evenings. The evenings when Marcus, so luckily, had never come to the factory to work on the accounts as he had done before. The evenings when Marcus, so fortunately, had almost never asked her out, though she had been so afraid that he would. The only time she had ever run into him by chance in the evening had been that time when she was leaving her evening class. He had known, of course, that she had the class on a Monday evening. But how much else had he known?

She had never thought about it at the time, but there had been so many coincidences. So many lucky breaks. So many times when Marcus, usually so determined, had unexpectedly backed off before she got herself into deep trouble. So many times when she had been terrified that he would find out. So many times when he hadn't.

Or had he? Was it possible, Janis asked herself, thunderstruck, that Marcus had actually known all along? That Marcus, always sharply observant, had seen all the telltale evidence of the Vane's contract? That he had known about the meetings with buyers on the days he didn't come to the factory? About the long evenings working with Stella on the samples? About the bundles of half-finished garments hidden at the back of the storeroom behind a façade of shirt boxes? About the dream she had nursed for so long, had wanted so fiercely that—at first, at least—she had been prepared to deceive him in order to make it come true?

He couldn't have known it all. The details of the contracts, the carbon copies she had hidden under her mattress, he couldn't have known all about those. But there was so much, she realised now, that he could hardly have helped seeing. There was so much that he could have discovered so easily, if he had only looked. If he had not looked, not seen what she didn't want him to see, it was idiotic and naïve of her to have imagined that it was pure luck that had kept it from him. He must have known. Except that, to her, he had pre-tended not to know.

Cheryl was kicking her hard under the table, and Janis, breaking away with difficulty from her train of thought, turned guiltily to the elderly accountant who had been waiting in vain for a reply from her. She would have to think about it later. But what a thing to think about! It was the last, the very last thing she had ever expected to discover.

Janis drove home from the Williamses' in a confused mixture of elation and despair. That Marcus should have known, and not said anything! He could only have done it, surely, out of love for her. But that he should then have been so angry when she told him, that he should have broken with her then, when there was no more secrets, nothing else to come between them—she couldn't understand it at all.

Peter and Cheryl were certainly not going to explain. She had lingered till the last guests had left, helped to load the dishwasher, and still been stonewalled, as if they had both agreed that the best way to deal with Cheryl's earlier slip was to pretend that it had never happened. There was only one thing to do. She would have to talk to Marcus himself.

Except that Marcus was still absolutely determined not to talk to her. It wasn't something she could write to him about, she had to see him face to face. Janis thought and thought. There was only one place where she could be sure of seeing Marcus, one place where he wouldn't be able to slip away from her.

She dressed, the next morning, in the mended green dress. She phoned Peter Williams as soon as she reached her office, and told him she was coming into town, and had to see him about something urgent. And when she was shown into Peter's office, at exactly ten-thirty that morning, she shut the door behind her and told Peter, very firmly, that she was determined to talk to Marcus, and if he refused to see her she was going to scream and shout and create hell right in the middle of Anson and Williams' big open-plan office.

'Janis! Janis, please.' Peter's face took on a pained look. 'Can't you just leave Marcus alone? Don't you think you've hurt him enough already?'

'*I've* hurt *him?*' Janis realised, from Peter's acute discomfort, that her voice was rising so loud, it was going to break the confines of his office. 'No,' she added more quietly. 'No, I haven't. All right, I have hurt him. I might hurt him a bit more this morning. But it'll be worth it, Peter. Believe me.'

Peter hesitated, and then went to the door. 'Marcus is going to hate me for this,' he said grimly.

'I'm sorry about that, Peter. Honestly I am. I couldn't see any other way.'

Peter threw her a despairing look as he walked out. Five minutes later he came back.

'OK,' he said. 'Try not to break the windows. They're very expensive.'

Marcus was standing by the windows, looking out at the sea. His back was to Janis as she slipped into his office, and his shoulders were set in a square way which spelled out acute hostility. She shut the door noisily so he'd know she was there, waited for a moment, and then decided that he had no intention of turning to face her.

She went to stand next to him. It was a hot day, and down on the beach she could just see the holiday-makers with their deckchairs and beach balls and windbreaks, frolicking around happily.

'When did you find out? About the Vane's contract?'

That got the reaction she was waiting for. With difficulty, she resisted the temptation to turn and meet his look.

Marcus sighed. 'The day after you signed it. The buyer phoned to check on the delivery dates, early, before you came in. I took the call.'

'You took all the calls,' Janis couldn't help saying. It was so obvious, now she knew. 'Why didn't you tell me then?'

He drew in his breath impatiently, and stalked across the room.

'What difference would it have made? Come on, Janis, what difference would it have made? You were so bloody determined. You'd have lied and cheated and deceived me in every way you could to get that damn contract. Wouldn't you?'

'Yes,' she admitted. 'Yes, just then I would have done. But you let me.'

'Oh, I let you. I covered for you all the way. I kept Anthea off your scent, and stayed away in the evenings, and buttered up that little buyer on the telephone. I tried to tell myself that it wasn't so bad, that at least I knew what you were doing, and it might have been worse if I hadn't known. And all the time I kept on thinking, tomorrow she'll tell me. Tomorrow she'll tell me. Except that you never damn well did.'

'Oh, Marcus, I couldn't. I just couldn't.'

'Of course you couldn't. You did every damn thing else, though, didn't you? You even went to bed with me to try to keep me sweet for long enough. I wanted you so badly, and I told myself that if we were lovers you'd be sure to tell me. But you never saw it like that, did you? It was never any more to you than a way to distract me, stop me from discovering what you were really up to.'

Janis went cold. 'You couldn't have thought that! Oh, darling, you couldn't have thought that.'

Marcus wasn't listening. 'Until it was too late. Until you thought it was too late for me to mess up your schemes. Then you waited just long enough to sort out a bolt-hole. You couldn't get away from me too soon, could you? You had to put as much distance between us as you could, the very first opportunity you got. I was still bloody foolish enough to dream of taking you to Paris, and all you wanted was to get away from me and stay away until I'd had a chance to clear out of your life. Well, I'm out. I'm out now. And I just damn well wish you'd keep away from me!'

'But you couldn't have thought—Marcus, didn't

you read my letter?'

'Get out. Please, Janis, get out. I don't want you crowing, and I don't want your thanks, and I can't bear to see you now. So please, please, get out. Go now.'

He had turned to the wall. And Janis, numbed and appalled and disbelieving, stood frozen by the window, unable to move, unable to think what to say to convince him how totally wrong he was.

She glanced wildly round the room. Peter's remark made her think of the window, but that was, she realised, a rather expensive way of attracting Marcus's attention. Finally she lit on an empty coffee-cup on the low glass table. She picked it up, and the saucer, and hurled them, very deliberately, one by one at the table.

The table, being very solid, didn't break, but the cup and saucer did, with a loud and satisfying smashing noise. Little splinters of china buried themselves in the thick carpet, the dregs of the coffee splashed across the table, and Marcus wheeled round abruptly. His eyes surveyed the damage and then came to rest on hers, wide open, momentarily defenceless.

'I—am—not—going.'

She could sense his temper begin to rise again, and she went on quickly, before it took him over.

'I'm not going. I'm never, never, *never* going! At least, not until I've explained. Not until you come with me.'

In the silence that descended, Janis somehow found the words to tell him how much she loved him. How wrong she had been about him, and how wrong he had been about her. What she had intended it to mean, when she had gone away, and how appallingly she had missed him, and how desperately she had wanted to see him and explain when she returned.

Marcus leaned against his overcrowded bookshelves, and listened until the flood of words dried up, and she waited tensely to discover if he had believed her.

'I couldn't bear it,' he said, 'if I found out you were lying now.'

Janis gave a shaky smile. 'To quote Louise,' she said, ' "you can only afford to be as cruel as this to people you love." '

Somehow, she found herself in his arms. He was holding her so tightly it hurt. And she wrapped herself around him, and melted against him, letting her body tell him how totally she longed to be his.

'I always knew,' he said, when he'd got his breath back, 'that your friend Louise was trouble.'

Janis reached out to brush his hair out of his eyes. 'You must have guessed that I'd be trouble, too.'

'Oh, yes.' Behind the unshed tears, his eyes were bright. 'I knew I was walking into trouble from the start. But I never guessed I'd fall headlong into it, the way that I did.'

'You were wonderful. I should have said it more often. I always thought you were wonderful.'

'You thought I was wrong!'

'You were! Weren't you?'

Marcus grinned. 'Just a little bit. But go on, admit it——'

'I was wrong, too!' Janis laughed. 'And a part of me knew it, all along. Next time, though, I'll trust you enough to believe you when you try to tell me so.'

'Now, wait a minute. Let's get this straight: I'm not coming back to Trenco. Trenco is yours, and it always will be. You need help in running it, but Peter can give you that, and Anthea, if you let her. You'll make mistakes, everybody does, but we're not going to spend our lives arguing about them. No, I'll stay here, and do my own work, and you'll stay at Trenco and do yours. And all the rest of our time we spend together. All right?'

'Very definitely all right,' agreed Janis, resting her head on his shoulder.

'Though I want you to have a sea view,' Marcus went on, thoughtfully. 'A view like mine. When we find somewhere to live, it must have a studio with big windows and a sea view. Unless you want to stay at White Gates?'

'No,' Janis said. 'White Gates was never really me. Mother knows I'll want to lead my own life somewhere else. And she's been determined, right from the day we met, that I should spend it with you.'

'Sensible lady,' Marcus agreed. 'And now we really ought to go and tell Peter that we've sorted out our differences.'

'Without breaking any windows,' Janis teased.

'Stupid bottle. Stupid bottle. Why won't it . . .'

Bruce eased, and then pushed, and then shoved, and then put the bottle between his knees and heaved on the cork. Whereupon it came out with a bang, sending him flying backwards, and Louise hurling herself forwards in a kind of rugby tackle on his legs, to rescue the champagne before it all soaked into her red carpet.

'More unpredictable than women, these things,' grumbled Bruce, as he filled their glasses.

'Perfectly predictable, darling. They just need handling gently and patiently. Otherwise they are liable to explode. Here, Janis.' Louise handed over an overflowing glass, with an expansive smile.

'I always knew we wouldn't be able to handle all this smoothly like Peter and Cheryl.'

'Honestly, Bruce, it's been a lovely evening,' Janis assured him. 'The best.'

It had been, too, in spite of the downpour on their way to the bungalow, and the burnt casserole, and the chocolate mousse that hadn't set. It was their third dinner, and they were all together and all happy, and, as Louise had said, if they were to have champagne next time, it would have to be babies, because they'd used the last of their excuses.

'Come on, Peter, you do the next bit, before we make a muck of that, too.'

'Coward,' teased Andy.

'Sorry, Bruce, it has to be you.'

Bruce shrugged. He shook the last drips from the second bottle of champagne into his glass, rose to his feet, waved the glass unsteadily in the air in front of him, and cried, 'To Marcus and Janis!'

'Oh, honestly, Bruce, how many times did I remind you, it's supposed to be——'

'Janis and Marcus!' roared the rest, as Louise's rugby tackle connected this time, and she and Bruce fell in a hilarious tumble on the floor.

Janis and Marcus. Marcus and Janis. It would be both, Janis thought happily, as she raised her glass to Marcus, and saw the reflection of Louise's dozens of home-made candles shining in his eyes. No winners, no losers, no bosses—just the two of them in partnership for ever.

'Paris for the honeymoon, then?' Roger asked them.

Marcus shook his head. 'It'll be November, remember, when Janis's next collection is safely out of the way. Paris can wait until we have a spring holiday. We'll honeymoon in Tunisia, we thought.'

'Lots of bright colours in Tunisia,' teased Louise.

'You must come and see the new sketches, Louise. And you, Cheryl. The Vane's buyer loved them. All bright reds and yellows and blues.'

'I loved them, too,' Marcus added loyally.

'Of course you did, darling.' Janis smiled. It had been Marcus who had insisted that she come to the dinner in her least successful garment ever, the green dress. He glanced down at it, and then met her eyes, telling her he remembered too, and telling her just how he would take it off her again, when the dinner was over and they were alone.

The doors in the Trenco factory was thrown open. The main doors, the doors to Janis's office, the big double doors that led through to the workroom. Only the storeroom doors were locked, protecting the last batch of coloured tops, all sewn and pressed and boxed and waiting to be delivered to Vane's warehouse the next day, and the shirts in their boxes, and the bales of brightly coloured cotton waiting to be made up into Janis's next collection.

Janis's sketches for the next collection, colour-washed in warm shades of red and orange and yellow, were pinned to the factory walls. The ceiling was festooned with the streamers that Stella and Deirdre and the other machinists had fastened up the night before, and with great bunches of balloons—red and orange and yellow. Janis was wearing a dress she'd designed herself, and Anthea and Stella and Deirdre and Jenny the new secretary and all the other Trenco staff were wearing her outfits. Marcus was in a Trenco shirt, and so was Matthew, amazingly—and under protest—and Bruce, and Peter, who had been voted head barman for the afternoon, as he definitely had the most reliable touch with the champagne.

Elizabeth Trench was wearing one of Janis's conservative beige dresses. None of the buyers had particularly liked it, but she had insisted that it was her favourite among Janis's designs. There was a new shine in her eyes, a new bounce in her walk since she'd sold White Gates and bought herself a flat down by the sea, and started a little part-time job at an estate agents in the town. She was smiling and animated as she talked to the assistant manager from the bank.

Everybody was there. The Vane's buyer, in a top from the last collection, which she had had to set aside quickly, she had told Janis, before they had all sold. Harry the maintenance man, and the security guard from the night shift. Anthea's plumber and Stella's Bill, happily established in his new job. The red-headed secretary from Anson and Williams, and the junior accountant who had been calling in once a week to help Anthea with the system. Roger and Emily, newly back from their own honeymoon—in Bognor, finally, but wonderful, they had assured Janis. Marcus's mother and father and his two younger brothers and his sister-in-law and his little nephew.

It was a success. A total, incredible, glorious success. Too good to last, perhaps. She knew she would have to watch her margins and keep an eye on delivery dates and check the cash-flow and allow for disasters for as long as she ran Trenco. But, at that very moment, Janis Trench had everything she had ever wanted.

And the next day, she would marry Marcus Anson in Smithbury Parish Church, in front of their families and friends and relations, and they would start a new life together. For a moment it all seemed a little too much, the crowded factory and the smiling faces and the pop of the champagne corks and the endless congratulations. When everybody seemed to be happily drinking and talking away, Janis sneaked off into the office, and gently closed the door behind her.

Marcus found her there a few minutes later; she was leaning on her desk, and looking at all the familiar plants and calendars and posters and filing cabinets.

'You've moved it back again,' he said.

She nodded. He hadn't been into her office for weeks; he had been staying away on purpose, she suspected, to convince her that he had meant what he said when he had promised not to interfere with Trenco again.

'It's Anthea's desk now. She's been so good, Marcus, with the accounts and the computer and everything. You wouldn't believe it.'

'I would,' he said gently.

'And Jenny sits over there, where Anthea used to be. The African violets are Jenny's.'

'Does she make a good cup of coffee?'

'Not bad. A little strong sometimes.'

She turned to meet his eye, and they laughed, and moved to hold each other.

'Oh, that first day you came here . . .'

'You were like a tomcat defending its territory. Fur out in all directions, claws at the ready . . .'

'Well, you were ready to attack!'

'I never meant it as an attack. You seemed so alone and so vulnerable, and I just wanted to protect you. Until I realised, too late, that you weren't willing to be protected.'

'No. No, I wasn't. I so badly needed someone to share the problems with, but I wasn't willing to be protected from them. I wanted a partnership, and you seem to be making a takeover bid.'

'I know, I know. Now I know.'

'Mother would like you back on the board, Marcus. As a family representative, nothing to do with the bank.'

He shook his head. 'I'll always be there to share the problems with you, you know that, but I'd rather leave things as they are, for now. And Peter's doing a good job, isn't he?'

'Of course he is. Dynamic, thrusting, aggressive young accountant . . .'

'What, Peter?'

Too late, she recalled that he hadn't been there when they'd joked about that at Louise's. But then, there would always be memories he didn't share, thoughts that were hers alone. There would have to be, if it remained a partnership and not a takeover.

'In his way,' she explained, a little lamely. 'I like them so much, Marcus. Peter and Cheryl. And your family are so nice, and . . .'

'And we're in love, and the world is a wonderful place.' He kissed her again. 'You still don't have to promise to obey tomorrow, you know.'

Janis laughed. He had been teasing her about that ever since she'd told the vicar she wanted the old-fashioned form of the marriage service.

'I know I don't have to. I wouldn't say it if I had to, but I *want* to say it. That's what makes it right. You can be the boss at home. I trust you not to take advantage of it too often!'

Laughing, Marcus pulled her close, and proceeded to take shameless advantage of it.

'Darling, they'll wonder where we've got to.'

'Rubbish! Everyone knows exactly where we've got to. You can go back in five minutes, and pretend to them all that it's the champagne that's given you that glow.'

'But darling, you're crumpling my best sample dress! Darling . . . darling . . .'

Step into a world of pulsing adventure, gripping emotion and lush sensuality with these evocative love stories penned by today's best-selling authors in the highest romantic tradition. Pursuing their passionate dreams against a backdrop of the past's most colorful and dramatic moments, our vibrant heroines and dashing heroes will make history come alive for you.

Watch for two new Harlequin Historicals each month, available wherever Harlequin books are sold. History was never so much fun—you won't want to miss a single moment!

 **Harlequin Romance**

Coming Next Month

Available in December wherever paperback books are sold,
or through Harlequin Reader Service:

In the U.S.
901 Fuhrmann Blvd.
P.O. Box 1397
Buffalo, N.Y. 14240-1397

In Canada
P.O. Box 603
Fort Erie, Ontario
L2A 5X3

"Barbara Delinsky has a butterfly's touch for nuance that brings an exquisite sheen to her work."
—*Romantic Times*

A nightmare begins for a young woman when she testifies in an arson trial. Fearing for her life, she assumes a new identity... only to risk it all for love and passion after meeting a handsome lawyer.

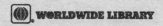

Harlequin American Romance

Romances that go one step farther...
American Romance

Realistic stories involving people you can relate to and
care about.

Compelling relationships between the mature men and
women of today's world.

Romances that capture the core of genuine emotions
between a man and a woman.

Join us each month for four new titles wherever paperback
books are sold.
Enter the world of American Romance.